Slugs slap ~~~ around Bol ~~~

He kept moving, incr~~~ ~~~nto the grass behind him, ~~~ ~~~ser than the first volley—and then he was surrounded by trees. The trunks and low branches shielded him as shots slammed into the timber, chewing bark and ripping at the foliage.

Overhead, the dark bulk of the hovering helicopter appeared. The men on the ground were waving it away, but the pilot ignored their pleas.

Bolan shouldered the MP-5, tracked the ground team and gave them a couple of short bursts—two went down, three others scattered.

As the chopper swung in toward the edge of the forest, Bolan edged around a tree, steadied his aim and let go with a long burst, concentrating on the helicopter's engine. The rounds hammered at the aluminum panels, punching ragged holes in the metal, as the Executioner held his finger on the trigger and cleared the magazine.

The chopper's power faltered, the smooth beating becoming ragged.

Bolan turned and ran deeper into the forest. The advantage was his, but he knew it wouldn't last. There were still the surviving members of the ground team, plus however many had been in the helicopter—an unknown figure at the moment.

The Executioner had a feeling that wouldn't remain a mystery for long.

Game on.

MACK BOLAN ®
The Executioner

The Executioner®
Don Pendleton's®

BLIND JUSTICE

A GOLD EAGLE BOOK FROM

WORLDWIDE.®

TORONTO • NEW YORK • LONDON
AMSTERDAM • PARIS • SYDNEY • HAMBURG
STOCKHOLM • ATHENS • TOKYO • MILAN
MADRID • WARSAW • BUDAPEST • AUCKLAND

If you purchased this book without a cover you should be aware
that this book is stolen property. It was reported as "unsold and
destroyed" to the publisher, and neither the author nor the
publisher has received any payment for this "stripped book."

First edition March 2012

Recycling programs
for this product may
not exist in your area.

ISBN-13: 978-0-373-64400-1

Special thanks and acknowledgment to
Mike Linaker for his contribution to this work.

BLIND JUSTICE

Copyright © 2012 by Worldwide Library

All rights reserved. Except for use in any review, the
reproduction or utilization of this work in whole or in part
in any form by any electronic, mechanical or other means,
now known or hereafter invented, including xerography,
photocopying and recording, or in any information storage
or retrieval system, is forbidden without the written permission
of the publisher, Worldwide Library, 225 Duncan Mill Road,
Don Mills, Ontario, Canada M3B 3K9.

This is a work of fiction. Names, characters, places and incidents are
either the product of the author's imagination or are used fictitiously,
and any resemblance to actual persons, living or dead, business
establishments, events or locales is entirely coincidental.

® and TM are trademarks of the publisher. Trademarks indicated
with ® are registered in the United States Patent and Trademark
Office, the Canadian Trade Marks Office and in other countries.

Printed in U.S.A.

The moral arc of the universe bends at the elbow of justice.
                              —Martin Luther King, Jr.
                              1929–1968

Without justice, this world would be lost. And when law and order is unable to establish it, I will be there to fight for those who have been wronged. Injustice will never go unpunished on my watch.

                              —Mack Bolan

THE
MACK BOLAN
LEGEND

Nothing less than a war could have fashioned the destiny of the man called Mack Bolan. Bolan earned the Executioner title in the jungle hell of Vietnam.

But this soldier also wore another name—Sergeant Mercy. He was so tagged because of the compassion he showed to wounded comrades-in-arms and Vietnamese civilians.

Mack Bolan's second tour of duty ended prematurely when he was given emergency leave to return home and bury his family, victims of the Mob. Then he declared a one-man war against the Mafia.

He confronted the Families head-on from coast to coast, and soon a hope of victory began to appear. But Bolan had broken society's every rule. That same society started gunning for this elusive warrior—to no avail.

So Bolan was offered amnesty to work within the system against terrorism. This time, as an employee of Uncle Sam, Bolan became Colonel John Phoenix. With a command center at Stony Man Farm in Virginia, he and his new allies—Able Team and Phoenix Force—waged relentless war on a new adversary: the KGB.

But when his one true love, April Rose, died at the hands of the Soviet terror machine, Bolan severed all ties with Establishment authority.

Now, after a lengthy lone-wolf struggle and much soul-searching, the Executioner has agreed to enter an "arm's-length" alliance with his government once more, reserving the right to pursue personal missions in his Everlasting War.

1

Seattle, Washington

"Okay, I know we can't kill him," Ken Brenner said. "Doesn't mean we can't make the bastard suffer. Put a bullet in him to slow him down. He's got something the senator wants and Kendal is a mean son of a bitch to say no to."

"Yeah? You know what pisses me off? That hard-faced mother he keeps at his side all the time. Stone." Steve Dunn hawked and spat with deliberate force. "Follows Kendal around like a fuckin' guard dog."

"Well, that's what he is. Senator Kendal's pet rottweiler."

Dunn folded his arms across his chest, hunching his shoulders against the chill rain sweeping in across the city. He was cold and he was wet, despite the supposed all-weather coat he was wearing. They had been waiting for almost an hour, watching the seedy hotel where their quarry was said to be staying. Brenner's informants had come up with the location earlier that afternoon, so he and Dunn had staked out the place and were waiting for their man to show.

"Jesus, Ken," Dunn complained, "why couldn't we have waited in the car?"

"We've been through this. If Logan sees our wheels parked on this street he's just liable to turn around and leave. He's a cop, Steve. A fucking good cop. He'd spot a car like ours with his eyes shut. Wrong vehicle for a deadbeat street like this."

"Yeah. Well, if I get a chill from this rain I'll send Kendal a bill for my medicine."

Brenner chuckled. "Good luck with that," he said.

"Hey, Ken, isn't that Logan?"

A man was walking along the sidewalk on the opposite side of the street. Brenner recognized him instantly. He watched Ray Logan as the cop headed for the hotel entrance. He tapped his partner and they crossed the street, coming up behind Logan.

The cop must have sensed them behind him. He turned, fixing his gaze on them. Brenner was shocked at Logan's appearance. His unshaven face was pale, cheeks sunken, his hair in need of a trim.

"Hey, Ray, where you been hiding?" Brenner asked. "You never call. You don't write."

"What the hell do you want, Brenner?"

"Isn't so much what we want, Ray," Brenner said. "It's Kendal who wants to have a talk with you."

The moment he heard the senator's name, Ray Logan threw himself at Brenner and Dunn. His move caught them off guard. They had expected him to run, not attack. His left shoulder rammed into Brenner's chest, taking his breath and knocking him off balance. Logan's right foot lashed out, catching Dunn in the groin, drawing a howl of agony from the man. As Dunn clutched at himself, Logan drove his fist into his face, drawing blood from Dunn's mouth.

"Get that bastard," Dunn said.

Logan had turned and now broke away from them, cutting across the street and making it to the dark mouth of an alley.

"Let's go," Brenner yelled, taking off after Logan, yanking his handgun from its holster.

Dunn followed, pawing at the blood oozing from his torn lip. He pounded after his partner, splashing through standing pools of water.

"Don't you fucking lose him," he called.

Up ahead he could see the dark outline of Logan, framed at the far end of the alley. There was a moment when it looked as if he had stopped running, half turning to look back at his pursuers.

Then he broke into motion, plunging out of the alley and into the street beyond.

THE MAN CAME OUT of the alley, cutting directly across the rain-swept street and was caught in the glare of the SUV's headlights. Tires squealed as the heavy vehicle violently braked, the forward motion arrested briefly as the rear end cycled around, the driver working the wheel with strong hands. It came to a rocking halt, the driver's-side window level with the fleeing man. There was a frozen millisecond where the two men held face-to-face.

The sharp crack of an auto pistol was followed by a blinking muzzle flash, a second shot was fired, and the fleeing man was slammed against the SUV's door. He tumbled away, going to his knees as the driver shoved open the door and exited the vehicle. He stood over the fallen man, a weapon filling his hands, and he returned fire in the direction of the two shadowed figures at the mouth of the alley. Whatever they might have expected, someone shooting back at them was not it. The shooter's slug slammed into the brickwork at the mouth of the ally, splinters peppering them, and without continuing the attack the men fell back into the dark maw of the gap between buildings.

Wind gusted in the deserted street, driving the rain forward in chilled sheets. It was close to 1:00 a.m. and the backstreet area of the city, never heavily congested even in daylight, was devoid of pedestrians in the early hours.

The SUV's driver leaned over and helped the wounded man to his feet. He opened the rear door and eased him inside the vehicle. He climbed back behind the wheel, dropped the lever into Drive and took the SUV away from the alley, making a fast turn, and headed for the city center.

"You okay back there?"

The wounded man had pulled himself to a sitting position.

Pain from his wounds was starting to make itself known and it took him a moment to speak.

"Been better," he said.

His rescuer glanced into the rearview mirror. He saw a gaunt face, eyes deep-set and dark-ringed. The hair plastered to the skull. Whatever had happened to the man had started well before the shooting. The problem was of long-standing.

"You need a hospital?"

"No hospital."

"You've got a couple of bullets in you," the driver said.

"Can't risk a hospital. They have to report gunshot wounds and details go on computers."

"You wanted by the police?"

The hoarse laugh from the rear seat held a cynical undertone. "Not in the way you might believe."

"How do I interpret that?"

There was a silence as the man reached inside his rain-soaked jacket. He held an object the driver could see in the mirror.

It was a black leather badge holder, and the streetlamps reflected off the metal of a shield that identified the Seattle Police Department.

"I'm a cop," the guy said. "The pair trying to bring me down were cops, too. Dunn and Brenner. I have something they want. My own squad captain, Fitch, is in on it, too. I was working undercover, on my own, and gathered one hell of a package of incriminating evidence against a guy named Kendal. Tyrone Kendal. And get this. He's a U.S. senator. Powerful man. Ruthless bastard. All started with a few rumors I got from one of my informants. Tied in with a case I was already working. So I turned my attention to Kendal and some of the lowlifes on his payroll. Didn't realize what I was into until I'd worked myself in deep. Spent a couple of months on it. Started to get results. Pictures. Video. Telephone voice recordings. Even managed to get into some of Kendal's computer files. The guy is into real nasty stuff. Blackmail. Bribery. He has a number of influential people by the balls. Other politicians. Business executives. Those three cops are banking payoff money—big bucks, too. One of my informants calls and tells me to get the hell out. Said I was blown. Next day they pulled his body out of the water. He'd been cut to pieces. I put my information together and checked into a hotel. Called my wife and told her to lie low until I had things sorted. I tried to bring one of the squad heads in on what I had. He reacted weird. I got the feeling he was working me. That was Fitch. Proved out when I found I was being followed. I managed to lose the tail, then realized the son of a bitch was working for the people I'd fingered. So I went off the grid. I'm trying to stay one step ahead while I try to figure out what to do. Who to trust now. When I called Rachel she warned me to stay away from the house. It was being watched."

There was a soft sound as the guy passed out and slumped across the rear seat. The driver decided his next move in seconds, turning the SUV at the upcoming junction and heading across town. He had made a swift decision, knew where he had to go, even though at that moment he had no idea where his choice would take him.

Be it by chance.

Fate.

A coming together of the two of them. He didn't know. All he was aware of was the wounded man in his vehicle. The guy carried a problem on his shoulders. And by stepping in he was now involved.

His commitment was dictated by his nature. The unspoken trait that seemed to bring him by time and place into direct contact with those in need of help.

And no one in such circumstances would ever be ignored by the driver of the SUV.

His name was Mack Bolan.

In a past time, in another place, due to his actions, he had been called Sergeant Mercy.

On that rain-swept night in Seattle that was the persona he

was channeling. But within a short time the twists and turns of life would click him into his other alter ego.

The Executioner.

Marty Keegan felt the cell phone vibrate in his pocket. He didn't need to check who was calling him because there was only one person who knew the number. The cell was a burn phone, purchased ten days ago when Ray Logan had taken himself off the grid and vanished. Keegan eased out of his seat, walking away from his desk and out of the squad room. As he reached the corridor outside he eased the phone from his pocket and keyed the button to accept the call.

"Hey, Ray," he said.

Logan's voice sounded tired. "I was ready to switch off," he said.

"Sorry, buddy. I had to get out of the squad room before I answered."

"You got anything for me?"

"Brenner and Dunn are acting like a couple of nervous old ladies. I'd be surprised if they're not in with Fitch. They're just standing around in a huddle and they break off if anyone goes near them. They came into the squad room last night looking like drowned rats. Dunn had a fat lip, like someone had punched him out. Don't know what they'd been up to."

"They were laying in wait for me near my hotel," Logan said. "Damn near let them take me, too. I slugged Dunn and managed to break away and run through an alley. Thought I was clear until I almost got myself run down. One of those bastards put a couple of slugs in me and I would have been finished if the driver of the SUV I ran into hadn't fired back at them, thrown me into his car and drove off."

"You hurt bad?"

"I've been in better health."

"Where the hell are you, Ray?"

"Not quite sure. Out of the city. I'm not being vague, buddy. I just don't know. I passed out a few times. When I came round the last time I was in a bed, bandaged up, hurting like crazy. The guy from the SUV told me the bullets had been removed. Racked up my shoulder some and one had cracked a couple of ribs. When I asked him he told me a doctor had dealt with me. Gave me blood. Pumped painkillers into me and left instructions that I wasn't to be moved for a few days. Said I had some kind of infection."

"Ray, you listen to yourself. This all sounds weird."

Keegan wasn't sure how to interpret what his partner was telling him. He had known Ray Logan for a long time—enough time to understand the man was not given to flights of fancy. If he heeded Logan's story it was because the man was straight down the line.

"It's true. On my life, Marty. It's all true."

"So who is this guy, Ray?"

"He doesn't give much away," Logan said. His voice was becoming softer, the words almost whispered. He paused to take a breath. "All I know, buddy, is he saved my life. He's in the kitchen making coffee right now."

"I got to ask, Ray. You trust this guy? I mean you…"

"Yeah, I trust him. Hard to explain but he makes it so you can't do anything *but* trust him. Something about the way he talks. I know I only met him a few hours ago, but…what the hell, Marty, the guy pulled my ass out of the grinder."

"You say he had a piece? Took a shot at Brenner and Dunn? I got to give him full marks for that. So what is he? Another cop? Some kind of Fed? Ray, he isn't setting you up is he? Playing games while he's really working for Senator Kendal?"

"Marty, if he worked for Kendal I wouldn't be calling

you like I am. I'd be tied to a chair while Kendal's lowlifes beat the shit out of me. This guy told me he works special assignments for some agency. Operates on his own. Marty, there was no way he knew I would show up when I did. Hell, I didn't know where I was going when I took off. I'm just grateful it happened." Logan went quiet for a minute. "You heard anything from Rachel and Tommy?"

"Sorry, pal. Nothing since I got them relocated. You know the way we played it. Out of the city. Way up country where she feels comfortable. No contact unless she makes it. I keep the location secret. Even from you."

"Damn."

"We have to keep this in play. You don't know where she is, so you can't spill. Until I can figure out how to get your evidence into the right hands we need to keep this way deep."

"I know. You realize what this is doing to me, Marty? If anything happens to them…"

"I'll keep Rachel and Tommy out of harm's way. Promise."

"Hell, I know you'll look after them…"

Logan's voice faltered, dying to a whisper. His body was forcing a shutdown. Weakness from his wounds and the effects of the painkillers.

"I won't give up on this, Ray. Look at it this way. Rachel is a smart girl. You told her to lose herself. That's what she's done. As long as she stays out of sight so does your evidence."

Keegan heard a low, mumbled whisper, then the phone cut off. He stared at his cell, then dropped it back in his pocket. "You hang in there, buddy."

Through the partition window of the squad room he could see that Dunn and Brenner were looking in his direction. He moved away down the corridor. The pair of cops were paying him too much attention. They knew he was not only Logan's partner, but a longtime friend. He was going to need to stay alert. Return the favor and keep *his* eyes on them.

3

"Marty is a good friend and partner. He was my backup when I was undercover. Rachel and I have known him a long time. You figure it out. Would I have trusted him with the safety of my wife and boy if I had doubts?"

"You make a good case," Bolan said. "You believe he's got your family safe?"

"Marty's smart. He'll have located them way out of the city."

"And what about your evidence? Will Rachel have it with her?"

Logan didn't reply immediately. Bolan saw he was fighting against the drugs and the infection. He let the cop have his time. It wasn't going to get him anywhere if Logan became too weak to talk. So Bolan sat back and waited.

"Man, that really caught me. Sorry."

"Don't apologize. If you need to rest longer, Ray, just tell me. You need the doc? Want me to call him in?"

"I'm good. I can't be sure what Rachel did with the evidence. She either took it with her, or hid it before she left. Maybe in our house."

"I can start there," Bolan said. "Eliminate that, then we can look at other options."

Logan managed a brief nod. "Okay, Cooper, I'll give you the address."

Bolan saw him sink back against the pillow, eyes closing.

The Executioner stood and quietly left the room to speak to the doctor before he left.

The medic was an old ally of Stony Man Farm. A man who understood Bolan's enduring struggle. He had experienced his own epiphany during a personal trauma and Bolan had come to his aid. The life-affirming philosophy that Bolan expressed, in actions rather than words, formed a bond between them that never needed expressing. Eric Madsen responded any time Bolan showed up. It wasn't the first time the Executioner had sought Madsen's help, and when he'd shown up with the badly wounded Ray Logan in the rear of his SUV, there had been no questions. Madsen took the wounded cop into his home office, ushered Bolan out of the treatment room and went to work. Logan was currently recovering, slowly, housed in one of the doctor's bedrooms and being tended by Madsen and his wife. When Bolan had explained the background and the possible threat to Logan, Madsen's wife, Laura, had smiled at him.

"You're trying to tell us this could put us in danger? Don't worry. You know how we feel about you, Coop, and how we can never repay you for what you did. So you just go out there and do what you do best. Leave that boy to get well. Find his wife and son, because that will help him get better faster than all the medicine Eric can offer."

THE LOGAN HOUSE stood back from the street. Timber and stone, well-maintained. A single garage attached to one side. Paved area for two cars. Bolan drove on by, passing three more homes before he took a right and parked out of sight. There was a wide alley running at the rear of the row. Bolan took it and made his way to the back fence of Logan's property. He checked the high gate, found it unlocked and slipped through. This kind of probe was better suited to the dark, but time didn't allow Bolan that luxury. He crossed the neat patio and reached the house. He saw immediately that the patio doors were breached—an inch gap told him someone had gotten inside.

Bolan unholstered the Beretta, easing off the safety. He slid the glass door open. The room inside had a wood-block floor. He noticed books disturbed on the shelves to his right. Furniture pushed out of place. A lampshade tilted. Moving quickly, avoiding any extraneous sound, Bolan reached the door, paused, listened. To his right, the open entrance hall and the front door. Directly across from the front door was the staircase leading to the upper floor.

He picked up a muffled voice. It came from upstairs. Bolan went up fast, the carpeted stairs deadening any sound. Movement on his left. A partly open door. A shadow disturbed the soft light. The same voice. Low, measured, not speaking English.

Bolan knew enough to recognize the language.

Russian.

Was the speaker talking to himself?

Or did he have a partner with him?

A thud as something was dropped to the floor.

This time a second voice. Remonstrating with the first man. This speaker was to the left of the door.

Whoever the men were they didn't belong in the Logan house.

Bolan took a step closer, ready to go through the door.

His intention was preceded as the door was wrenched open and a dark-clad figure appeared, a stubby SMG slung from his left shoulder. The guy had his head turned away from Bolan as he said something to his partner.

So much for the stealth approach, Bolan thought.

Then used the clear moment to his own advantage. As the visible man stepped through the door, head swiveling to the front, seeing Bolan and reaching for the SMG, Bolan swept the Beretta round in a brutal, clubbing action. It slammed against the man's skull with a sodden thud. The gunman uttered a shocked gasp, sagging against the door frame, and Bolan struck again—same place, even harder. Blood spouted, rushing down the man's face and soaking into the sweater he was wearing. As he began to slump, Bolan shouldered him

back into the room, already picking up the thump of foot-
steps as the second guy ran forward. He sensed the movement seconds before he saw the man. Big, his broad shoulders
and barrel chest topped by a shaved, short-necked head, he
moved with a solid gait. Bolan had no chance to raise his
weapon. The large figure loomed close, muscular arms and
wide hands reaching for him. Bolan lowered his own shoulders, turning slightly and hit the guy in his midsection, not to
halt him, but to use the other's forward momentum to propel
him across Bolan's back. Bolan thrust upward and the big
Russian was hurled over his back, feet leaving the floor. The
big man uttered a startled cry as he was launched through the
air. Bolan turned about in time to see the Russian slammed
against the wall, plaster shattering under the impact. Framed
pictures were shaken from the wall as the man crashed to
the floor in an ungainly tangle. Bolan stepped in close, ready
as the Russian started to rise. He timed it so that as the man
swayed on his legs, Bolan drove his right knee in hard. It
caught the guy under the thick jaw. The Russian grunted,
blood spurting from between his lips as his teeth snapped
together and sliced into his tongue. He toppled back, eyes
glazing, as he bounced off the wall and into Bolan's knee a
second time. The brutal impact put him down with a sub-
dued crack as his neck and upper spine snapped. The big man
dropped with the looseness of death.

Behind Bolan the first guy was struggling to recover himself, groping for the SMG hanging from his shoulder. The
big American turned fully. He saw the SMG tracking in, the
guy's finger already on the trigger. No hesitation as Bolan
brought the 93-R on line and punched a triple burst that took
away the left side of the man's skull in a glistening spray.
The Russian toppled back, eyes wide from shock as he hit the
carpeted floor on his back.

"Damn," Bolan muttered at the way it had gone.

He was less concerned with the Russians' deaths than he
was with the probable outcome once their principals found
out what had happened. The would-be shooter had placed

himself in the firing line once he went for his weapon. He had gambled and lost. Rules of the game. But there was someone behind the pair who had invaded Logan's house, plainly looking for something, and that someone was not going to be pleased to learn his men had been discovered and taken out.

As he frisked the two men Bolan was questioning the presence of Russian heavies in the equation. How did they fit into what Ray Logan had unearthed?

A U.S. senator involved with Russians? Bolan let the question lie as he discovered two wallets, a pair of Russian passports and a vehicle key with a rental fob attached. The fob had the license-plate number on it. Bolan pocketed the items.

Neither of the Russians had a cell. Unusual, but not unheard of. Perhaps they had a phone installed in their vehicle.

Bolan called Stony Man Farm on *his* cell, connected with Aaron "the Bear" Kurtzman.

"Hey, we figured you were on your way home. Didn't you finish your mission?"

"Yeah. But something new came up and I need your help."

"Can't get along without me, can you, Striker?" Kurtzman grumbled amiably.

"It would be a struggle," Bolan said.

"Give me the details."

Bolan gave Kurtzman the number from the key fob and the passports. "See what you can come up with."

"Be in touch," Kurtzman said.

Bolan took a tour of the house. Checked it thoroughly, including all the places Logan had suggested. He found nothing, figuring that as the Russians had still been looking they hadn't unearthed anything themselves. The more he searched, the less he believed Rachel Logan had used her own home to hide her husband's evidence, and the more convinced he became that she had taken it with her when she left for her secret location.

He exited the house after a half hour, closing the patio doors behind him and returned to his own rental. He fired up the motor and drove on, cruising the back lane until he was able to rejoin the main road. Bolan headed back in the general direction of the city center, spotted a diner and drove in and parked. He went inside and ordered a coffee. He took his cell out and called Logan's burn phone, indentifying himself to the cop.

"You had visitors. They were looking for something in your house, too. There was nothing to find. Place is clean."

"Trying to get a line on my evidence and my family. Rachel wouldn't leave any trace. You get an ID on them?"

"Work on this, Logan. They were Russian. Had passports to prove it."

"*Russian?* What were Russians doing in my house?"

"I'm having that checked out now."

"Where are the perps?"

"Still at your house, but not in a position to leave on their own two feet. They didn't take too well to being interrupted."

"I'm trying to figure out how a pair of Russians are involved." Logan paused, his thoughts slowed by the effects of the sedatives and his weakness. "Hey, Cooper, I'm getting some recall here. I almost lost it. I did come up with a Russian connection during my investigation. A guy Kendal had contact with. Can't make it any clearer at the moment. Hell, why did I forget that?"

"When we get some identification maybe we'll get an answer to that," Bolan said. "In the meantime, don't beat yourself up if you can't pull all the details into the open. Ray, you just let me know if you hear anything about or from Rachel."

"I will. Cooper, she's gone to ground so it's not going to be easy finding her. Rachel knows how to survive. Before we were married she did three years as a Park Ranger upstate. It was how we met. I was following up on a murder inquiry that took me out of the city. Rachel had found a body that had the earmarks of the perp we were after. Her intel helped us track the guy down."

"Now that's a romantic way to meet your future wife," Bolan said.

"Tell me about it. Happened between us before we knew what hit us. I figure that's what Keegan has done. Sent her somewhere up country. And Rachel hasn't lost any of her outdoor instincts, Cooper. She's at home out there."

"So she can handle herself?"

"Oh, yes."

"What about weapons?"

"That girl can shoot. Just don't ever get her mad if there's a 9 mm in the same room."

"Would she favor the part of the country she patrolled when she was a Ranger?"

"Maybe, but Keegan isn't about to let on where. It's a big piece of freehold, Cooper. Runs all the way up to the Canadian border."

After ending the call, Bolan ordered fresh coffee, then decided he might as well eat, given this enforced downtime. The old military maxim.

Eat when the opportunity presents itself.

Sleep on the same premise.

The combat soldier's credo. Never waste free time. Use it like it's going out of fashion. Grab it with both hands. Make the most of this day and let tomorrow catch up when it can.

He turned his thoughts to the man who seemed to be the driving force behind Ray Logan's problems.

Senator Tyrone Kendal.

Bolan tried to imagine what was behind the man's desperate actions. Why did he want so badly to get hold of Logan and the evidence that the cop claimed to have gathered?

Must have been something damning. Something that had pushed the senator into such a flurry of activity.

Armed teams searching for Logan.

Bad cops shooting at him.

And Russian heavies invading the man's home.

KURTZMAN'S CALL CAME just as Bolan got back in his vehicle. He put the cell on speaker and listened to the rundown on the Russians.

"Couple of heavy hitters. Ivan Tupelov and Mako Sheranova. Suspected of a number of crimes but never proved. They showed up on U.S. and international databases. They work for a dubious character named Maxim Koretski. If it's illegal this lovely guy has his hands in it. Trafficker in everything murky. Runs a number of clubs here and in Russia—guy gets around. But he's so lawyered-up he's bulletproof. We dredged up a few articles from newspapers and magazines. This guy is seriously into big-time crime. Suggestion is he wants to be Mister Big. In the past a couple of his near rivals have been mysteriously eliminated. No proof, but the finger points Koretski's way."

"Any connection at all to a Senator Tyrone Kendal?"

"He in this deal, as well?"

"I think so, but right now I can't figure the why. I'm just trying to connect the dots."

"I'll keep checking. The car detail panned out. A rental paid for through one of Koretski's *legitimate* businesses."

"Thanks, Bear. Come back anytime you dig up anything."

"You got it, Striker. What's next for you on this?"

"Collateral damage. I need to cut away some of the trash."

4

It was no secret that Senator Tyrone Kendal enjoyed the good things in life, and he made sure everyone around him understood that. Kendal tolerated no deviation from his desires or his expensive lifestyle. Only the best was good enough— home, possessions, his cars. It helped that he was a wealthy man. He had inherited the Kendal fortune on the death of his father, a man who had worked his way up from a menial job as a dirt farmer to become the head of a multinational company encompassing oil, copper-mining and a manufacturing base providing products as diverse as home appliances to electronics for the IT industry. Tyrone Kendal the younger inherited the companies and the money, but unfortunately he lacked the people skills. He assumed the mantle of top dog, but in doing so he became arrogant, self-important and unfeeling.

So it was a surprise when he entered politics. He abandoned his commercial interest in the slew of companies, handing over the reins to his previous second-in-command, and presented himself as a man free of business connections. But that was for public consumption only. The truth was that Kendal still maintained control of the businesses. It was all done through a layered facade of shell companies, corporate subterfuge and a legion of lawyers. As far as the world in general understood, Kendal had stepped down, distanced himself from the business enterprises and had become a man of the people. He devoted himself to his new calling, and with the skill that had created his business empire, he entered politics and surprised everyone with his early successes. That surprise was compounded when he eventually became a U.S. senator, due in great part to the unstinting efforts of the team he built around him. They portrayed him as a caring, honest man who represented the *people*. He spent lavishly on the things that mattered, not sparing himself during the rallies and the election hustings. He travelled the state of Washington, where his main dwelling was situated, enduring the long days and nights of meeting his constituents. He listened to their needs, promised them whatever they asked for, smiling and waving, then returned to his home and wiped the smile away, downed expensive whiskey and swore if he ever had to listen to another request for help he would take out his shotgun and blow the bastards' heads off.

Kendal won his election by a landslide. Two days later he left for D.C. to take up his seat and became a thorn in the opposition party's side. He understood how to play the game. He cultivated the right friends using his dominant personality. He made enemies, too, but that was something Kendal thrived on. He fought his corner, quickly learning to make the cards fall the way he wanted.

That had been eight years ago. These days he was a major player in the political circle, able to take on anyone who stepped into the ring. His reputation as a tough, uncompromising opponent had won him few friends. His hard-edged stance distanced him from many. Kendal maintained his arm's-length persona. He had his own agenda to pursue and keeping people at bay allowed him to concentrate on that. He did not like to be faced with anything that might harm his career.

Over and above all else was Kendal's driving force, the one thing that mattered to him. Greed. Plain and simple. No amount of financial success was ever enough. He needed more. Much more. Because immense wealth also brought its own agenda. Wealth begat power, and limitless power was Kendal's desire. Power, control, the narcotic that demanded endless feeding. He had reached that stage where the craving had become almost self-sustaining. But Kendal would never consciously admit, even to himself, that his need was unstoppable.

And after all this hard work, it frustrated him that a lowly Seattle cop was making an attempt to thwart him.

"This Seattle cop, he's still causing us problems?" he asked. He was like a headmaster interrogating a failing pupil. "Why hasn't he been dealt with?"

"He's disappeared."

Kendal cleared his throat. "*Disappeared?* Penn and Teller style, in a puff of smoke? Levitated into an alien saucer?"

Eddie Bishop, the man facing Kendal across the senator's expansive desk, looked uncomfortable. In fact, he *was* uncomfortable. Confronting Kendal with bad news was never a pleasant experience. Kendal did not like to be delivered bad news. It meant someone was not doing his job right. If you took the senator's money you damn well better earn it.

"He's just dropped out of sight."

"What about the wife and kid? They magically vanished, too?"

Bishop winced inwardly. At that moment he was wishing *he* could drop out of sight.

"Logan must have got to her before our people. She's gone, as well. But we're working on it."

"Right. *Working* on it. That's a great comfort to me." Kendal slammed his clenched fist down on the desk, his handsome face flushing with anger. Objects on the desk jumped in the air. "I can't believe I'm hearing this crap. You understand what's riding on this? I'll fucking tell you. The whole goddam operation is riding on this. If that white-knight cop gets someone to listen to him and we get investigated, we all go down the crapper—Koretski included. And the last thing we want is Maxim Koretski pissed off. You think *I'm* a bastard—think on."

"Senator, we're doing our…"

"Do not say your best, because if you were, Logan would

be down in my basement begging for a bullet in the back of his skull. If you were doing your best, his wife and kid would be strung up in front of him dripping blood on the floor. Now, is that what's happening?"

"No, sir."

"At least we agree on that. So get off your butt and call your people. Make them understand that money and people are not a problem. Use those things to get me results. I want Seattle searched top to bottom. Use your street informers. Dig that bastard out of whatever hole he's crawled into and get that information from him before he uses it. Close the city down for him. Shut off communication. I want you to beg, borrow, blackmail everyone you can think of. You understand, Bishop? Ray Logan doesn't know it yet, but he's already a dead man."

"I'll get right on it."

As Bishop made for the door Kendal said, "Tell Stone I want to speak to him as soon as he arrives."

Bishop experienced an involuntary shiver at the name. If Kendal was sending for Vigo Stone then someone was in major trouble. Kendal only used Stone when he had a special assignment that needed handling. Bishop hoped his name didn't come up in the conversation.

5

His name was Vigo Stone. He worked for Senator Tyrone Kendal. His job demanded he be available 24/7. Kendal had a direct cell-phone line to the man if they were not in hailing distance of each other—which happened from time to time when Stone was working a special assignment. Those around Kendal viewed Stone with caution. The man was not the kind who would be termed *sociable*. He displayed a remoteness that kept men at a distance and females feeling uneasy. None of that had the slightest effect on Stone. He worked for the senator, but not for his official position.

Stone was around forty. A man of medium height, lean and with the presence of a prowling big cat. His quiet demeanor matched his looks. A hollow-cheeked face with a slim, slightly hooked nose and wide, thin lips. His eyes never rested. They moved constantly, seeing everything, probing, curious. His smooth skull was shaved, the skin showing a faint sheen. He dressed well. Always in a suit, tie and immaculate shirt.

He entered Kendal's office and sat facing the senator's desk. No words were exchanged until Stone had fully read the slim file Kendal passed to him.

"I take it there has been no success finding Logan? Or his wife and brat?"

"Nothing. Bishop and his people have found nothing."

"Bishop? The man's a dinosaur. He has no idea.".

"Which is why I want you to handle this. Do what you

do best, Vigo. You take charge. Run it however you damn
well want. Bishop will take orders from you directly. Hire
who you need. Pay off who you want. I want this to go away
before it bites us all in the ass. I'll do what I can to keep
Koretski at arm's length."

"Koretski has dealt himself in?"

"He has a vested interest. He is my partner in this venture.
Hell, more than a partner. If Logan's information falls into
the wrong hands we're all going down the toilet, Vigo. And
there are a lot of important people in the mix. So we need to
suppress anything that damn cop has dredged up."

"You know how I work, Senator. No interference. No di-
rectives. I run my own show."

Kendal smiled. "Vigo, I don't need reminding, and I have
no worries on how you do your job. Never have in the past,
so why should things be different this time? You will have
access to the open-ended account as usual and we will settle
up when it's all over."

"Is there any current information not in the file?"

"Our pet cop, Captain Fitch, informed me his two blood-
hounds, Brenner and Dunn, passed along something that
might be useful."

"Brenner and Dunn—the pair that let Logan run?"

"Not their finest hour," Kendal said.

"I'm surprised they can stand up and walk without the
need of an instruction book. So what was their information?"

"One of the cops in the squad is a close friend of Logan.
He's also Logan's partner. Name of Marty Keegan. Dunn and
Brenner have a feeling he's been in contact. Couple of times
he's taken cell-phone calls and been cagey about anyone listening in. Could be nothing, but on the other hand maybe
not."

"It's a start," Stone said. "I'll need details. Keegan's home
address. Anything that might help."

Kendal nodded. "No problem," he said. "Give it a half
hour and I'll have all there is to know about Lieutenant Marty
Keegan."

"Good." Stone stood, adjusting his jacket. "I'll need a vehicle."

Kendal picked up the internal phone. He spoke to one of his assistants. "Bring it around to the front in half an hour," he said finally. He nodded at Stone. "Fixed. Anything else?"

"I'll wait for the Keegan information in the library."

"You want tea?" Kendal asked.

"Why not," Stone said and left the office.

Kendal picked up the phone again and instructed refreshments be sent to Stone. The man only ever drank tea. He never touched coffee or alcohol. Come to think of it, Kendal mused, the man didn't smoke, rarely smiled and only spoke when it really mattered. He wondered how Stone related to women and sex. What the hell, Kendal decided. The man was good at his job. That was all he was concerned about.

TWO HOURS LATER Stone was on the road behind the wheel of a high-spec Chevy Impala, sitting in quiet comfort as he negotiated the traffic. The satnav system was directing him to Marty Keegan's address as he was already planning his course of action. He understood what needed doing. The senator had a crisis on his hands. One that had the potential of destroying his world and himself. As far as he was able, Stone would take steps to prevent that from happening. His association with Kendal went back a number of years and over those years Stone had engineered a number of what he termed *rescues* on behalf of the man.

Tyrone Kendal was a powerful man. A good friend, in the loosest sense of the word. He expected total loyalty from his people and in return he looked after them and paid generously. On the other hand he was not a man to cross or threaten. When that happened, Kendal struck out with considerable force. He would not tolerate any kind of attack on himself personally, or on the grandiose plans he involved himself in. To help in reducing threats to a minimum, Kendal had a tight group around him—advisors, lawyers and specialists in a number of skills, many of them with dubious pedigrees.

And his ultimate weapon.

Vigo Stone.

In his ethereal world, Stone's rivals referred to him as *The Enforcer.* His reputation preceded him. Hard men, no beginners themselves, walked around Stone. They measured their words in his presence. He was not given to loose talk, especially about himself. There was no need. Those in the know were fully aware of his past deeds, and none of them had any desire to find they were under his eye. As much as possible they stayed well clear.

MARTY KEEGAN LIVED near Seattle's waterfront in one of a number of older buildings converted into separate residences. Rolling the Chevy along the street, Stone passed the address, then turned down a side street that let him view the rear of Keegan's building. Easy access and exit from the place. At the end of the block Stone spotted a parking lot and drove in. He paid for the maximum stay and displayed the ticket on the dashboard of the Chevy before lifting his laptop computer bag off the rear seat. He locked the Chevy, slung the bag from his left shoulder and casually walked out of the parking lot, turning down the sidewalk that would eventually return him to the front of Keegan's place.

He shifted the computer bag on his shoulder. There was no laptop in the bag. It held Stone's work kit, as he called it. The tools of his trade.

The information Kendal had supplied detailed, among other things, Keegan's current shift timetable. The cop was due to finish in a half hour and unless he had other plans he would drive home. Stone acknowledged that fact was one he could not plan for. He was going to have to wing that part. But he had great faith in human nature, accepting the predictable and understanding the regular routine of peoples' lives.

He strolled along the street, eyeing the building he was heading for. At this time in the afternoon the majority of people were still at work, so there were only a few around. Stone had been banking on that. He needed to get into the building and then Keegan's apartment. He knew the location—ground floor, just along from the front entrance. There were two other ground-floor apartments. The one immediately adjacent to Stone's was occupied by an elderly woman who lived on her own and rarely left the building. The other, across the hall from the Keegan apartment, belonged to a young single businesswoman who worked long hours and seldom came home before seven in the evening. Stone had no idea how Kendal had obtained such detail, but he admired the man's thoroughness and professionalism. The details made Stone's entrance a little less hazardous. When he reached the building he walked calmly along the short path, up onto the porch and in through the open front door. It was quiet inside the shaded lobby. Stone didn't waste time surveying the scene. He went directly to Keegan's door, pulled a pair of latex gloves from his jacket, took a set of expensive lock picks from another pocket in his jacket and had the door open within twenty seconds. Inside he closed the door again and stood for a few moments absorbing the apartment setup. Once he had it fixed in his mind he stepped into the kitchen, laid his bag on the counter and opened it.

The kitchen window was shaded with slatted blinds and looked out on the street. Stone made sure he was not silhouetted on the window as he laid out his implements on a towel he unrolled across the counter. That done, he filled a hypo syringe from a bottle.

Then he stood to one side of the kitchen window where he could see the street.

And patiently waited for his victim.

Marty Keegan.

Seattle cop.

Partner and good friend of Ray Logan.

The man who was going to tell Stone everything he might know, imagined he knew, about the runaway cop and his family.

It might take a half hour. It might take longer. But in the end Keegan would give it all up.

They always did.

It was not arrogance on Stone's part. It was fact. He had worked interrogations many times before, and of one thing he was sure. They always gave up the information.

No one could withstand interrogation indefinitely. There would come a point when human tolerance to pain in its infinitely varied forms became too much. Then the victim would tell Stone whatever he needed to know simply to make it all stop. It had to happen. There was nothing surer. Just like sunrise and sunset—no deviation.

It would happen.

There was a phrase from a well-known TV series that Stone liked for its simple, crystal clarity.

Resistance is futile.

That was how it would be for Lieutenant Marty Keegan.

6

Stone heard the sound of a key being inserted into the lock. He moved quickly to stand behind the door, the syringe in his right hand, his left ready to clamp over Keegan's mouth. He was calm, as always, his control absolute. The door clicked and swung inward, briefly obscuring Stone's view. He'd expected it so it didn't faze him. Keegan stepped inside, turning to close the door, and his gaze settled on Stone's waiting form. Stone nudged the door shut, heard the latch click into place, and in the same movement he stepped in close to the startled cop, left hand coming down on the man's partly open mouth. His right brought the hypo forward, his swift jab driving the needle into the soft part of Keegan's neck just below his jawline. The plunger depressed and the hypo's contents were injected into Keegan. Stone used his bulk to push Keegan against the wall, holding the man immobile for the few seconds it took for the syringe's contents to spread and take effect. Keegan's eyes widened, rolling in their sockets. He made a breathy sound and Stone took his hand from the cop's mouth. Keegan began to go down, his limbs losing all control. Stone held him by his jacket, letting the man slump to the floor. Safe in the knowledge the cop would be unconscious for some time, Stone went back into the kitchen and put the hypo back in its case.

Stone went through Keegan's pockets, placing everything he found on the kitchen counter, including Keegan's badge and Beretta auto pistol. The cop's phone was turned off and placed in the computer bag. Stone emptied Keegan's wallet—nothing unusual except for $150 in cash. Stone pocketed that. Returning to the sprawled form, Stone dragged Keegan across the living room and into the bedroom. Using a thin-bladed scalpel from his bag, Stone cut away Keegan's clothing, took off his shoes and socks, then hoisted the naked cop on top of the bed. Using plastic ties he tethered Keegan's ankles and wrists to the head and foot posts, completing his task by sticking a strip of duct tape over the man's mouth.

Then he waited. He knew the strength of the injection and was rewarded when Keegan started to come round within three minutes of his estimated time. Still groggy, Keegan struggled against his bonds, mouthing from beneath the duct tape. After a few minutes, exhausted, Keegan became still, his eyes fixed on the patiently waiting Stone.

"All done? I could have told you struggling would only tire you out, but you decided to find out for yourself." Stone allowed himself a rare smile. "I have no idea what your sexual preferences are, Marty. Maybe you've already tried bondage, maybe not. In any case, being restrained can be quite a unique experience—but I'm sure you never expected it to turn out like this.

"We have ourselves a problem, Marty. Your good friend Ray Logan has something my principal wants very badly, which I'm sure you realize. Ray has gone undercover. His wife, Rachel, and his son, Tommy, have also vanished. My job is to locate Logan's wife. I don't contemplate failing to do that. To be truthful I have never failed and don't expect to start now. As Logan is not immediately available, I need to get my hands on Rachel and Tommy, and that is where you come in, Marty. I have reliable information that you may have been talking to Logan on your cell phone. Not very smart to do that in the precinct. But it places you in the position of being Logan's confidant. So, I think you may have the information I'm looking for."

Keegan's head shook from side to side, his eyes giving away his thoughts.

"My problem, Marty, is an inability to accept things on face value. Your denial doesn't convince me. So we are going to have to rectify that. As you don't seem to be in an obliging mood it's going to have to be messy." Stone moved away from the bed, pausing at the door. "How is your pain threshold, Marty?"

When Stone returned from his visit to the kitchen he held a fine-edged scalpel in one hand and a pair of metal pincers in the other. He stood over Keegan and displayed the instruments.

"One cuts, one tears, Marty. Let's see which has the greater effect on you."

It took less than twenty minutes for Marty Keegan to give up what he knew. Within that time period he passed out twice and Stone had to wait until he came round. Stone was not surprised at how quickly the man submitted. The scalpel and the pincers were crude, simple tools. They performed well though. By the time a sweating, shivering Keegan capitulated, his naked body was bloody and cut open. The bed sheets where he lay were sodden with blood.

"Ready to talk?" Stone asked.

A frantic nod.

Stone put aside the instruments he had been using. He produced a Cold Steel Tanto knife and showed it to Keegan.

"Let me explain how this will go. I remove the tape from your mouth so you can tell me what I need to know." He took a compact digital recorder from his pocket and held it for Keegan to see. "You speak into this. I will have this knife on your throat. If you even attempt to yell a warning I will simply cut your throat wide open, and believe me, this knife is sharp enough to sever your head. The decision is yours, Marty. Give me what I want and you could survive this. Trick me and you die. No screaming sirens will get here in time to save you. Make your choice."

Keegan nodded.

The recorder was switched on. The knife blade was placed against Keegan's throat. Lightly, but even the gentle pressure was enough to cut the skin. Keegan felt the duct tape peel away, exposing his mouth. He stared up into the cold, expressionless eyes of his tormentor.

"Are we good, Marty?"

"Yes." His words came out in a raspy whisper.

"Tell me where they are."

Keegan made his confession, the words tumbling over one another in his desperation to get it all out.

"Better be right, Marty. Or it's going to be more of the same."

"It's the truth. For God's sake, I'm telling you the truth."

Stone nodded as he pocketed the recorder. "I believe you, Marty."

"You'll let me go? You said…"

"Marty, understand me, this is best for both of us."

The Tanto's blade cut down and across. The stroke was delivered with intense force, cutting off any sound Keegan was about to make. His body arched up off the bed, bending bowlike against his tethered limbs. In the instant before blood started to spurt Stone stepped away from the side of the bed, distancing himself from the arcing fountain of red. He watched for a few seconds, turned and made his way to the kitchen where he placed his instruments back in the computer bag and zipped it closed.

He opened the apartment door and peered out into the lobby, seeing no one. Somewhere in the building he picked up the sound of a radio playing music. He closed and secured the door, then turned down the passage that led to the rear of the residence and let himself out into the yard. He walked by the line of trash cans, slipped out through the rear gate and walked along the quiet access road. Stone returned to the parking lot and unlocked his car. He placed the computer bag on the seat beside him, started the Impala and reversed out of his spot. He drove out of the lot and back to the road that would take him away from the area. He had only been driving for a few minutes when it started to rain again. Stone settled in his seat. The rain drummed on the roof of the car, making a comforting sound. Stone had always liked that sound. Today he enjoyed it more than usual.

7

Eddie Bishop was not pleased with the way the chain of command had changed. Until Vigo Stone showed up, Bishop had been Kendal's main man. He had been demoted to second place. He didn't like it, but there wasn't a damn thing he could do about it. He wasn't about to go whining to the senator, and he was for sure not going to let his feelings show in front of Stone. The man had a reputation no one would stand up and challenge. Anyone and everyone who knew about Stone was aware of his past—what he had done, what he was supposed to have done. There were some stories that edged on the fanciful. Bishop's contact with the man was minimal, but even that had been enough to convince him of the truth behind the tales. He believed Stone capable of any atrocity. Stone brought something to the party that was less than human. There was an aura following him around. The man had little personality. He silenced a room when he walked in. His manner struck Bishop as *creepy*. It was the only word to describe the man.

When Bishop was summoned to Kendal's office, following Stone's return from Seattle, it was to be told where to send his team.

Kendal told the assembly that Stone had been to talk with Marty Keegan, one of Logan's cop friends, and he had divulged the whereabouts of Logan's wife and son. The senator was obviously pleased with the results of Stone's mission. He sat back as Stone gave the orders on what they would do to retrieve Rachel and Tommy Logan.

"We need them alive," Stone said. "The woman might know where Logan has hidden the information he collected. Let's make sure we find her."

Kendal tapped his desktop with his knuckles, drawing attention to himself. He leaned forward, stroking one lean hand through his thick mane of silver hair.

"Vigo has made up for our lack of intel. Let us not screw this up. Take this to heart, gentlemen—Vigo Stone runs the operation as of now. Listen to him. Follow his orders. It's time we brought this situation back under our control. We need to find Logan. We need to find his wife and son. And most of all we need to get our hands on that damn file of information, because if we let it get into the wrong hands we are all, and I mean *all,* heading for the dumper."

The senator sat back, raising a hand in Stone's direction so he could carry on with his briefing.

"Rubin, Madden, Burdett. I want you to make the run to the cabin. Take Lohman as your wheelman. Don't make the mistake of thinking this will be easy. Logan's wife used to be a Park Ranger. That means she knows the forest. She was trained to handle a gun. Step out of line and she *will* shoot you. Most likely in the balls. She has her kid with her and she'll fight to protect him. A mother protecting her young is a hell of an animal. Make sure you wear comsets so you can stay in contact with each other once you're in the forest. Try and make a silent approach. Surround the cabin and spot your target before you move in. This might sound like overkill to some of you hotshots. Don't be fooled—it's not. Once something starts it can go from zero to shit in a heartbeat. If it does, you can lose the advantage so fast it'll make your head spin. That's when you get casualties. We do not want the Logan woman harmed. If she ends up badly hurt or dead, then we are back where we started. And then I am not going to be a happy man."

When are you ever a happy man? Bishop thought, but he kept it to himself because he knew Stone meant every word.

"We will back up the ground team with extra men who will follow from the air. A helicopter is being prepared as we speak. The rest of you cover the city streets—find Logan. Use every source available. Bishop, talk to those Keystone Cops we have on the payroll. Remind them what they're being paid for. And make it doubly understood they are as deep in this as any of us."

Bishop spotted Kendal watching him out of the corner of his eye. Wanting to see how his lieutenant was handling his *demotion,* he supposed. He maintained a neutral expression, nodding in Stone's direction.

"I'm on it," he said.

"Don't be on it," Stone said. "Be ahead of it."

Bastard, Bishop thought. The man couldn't resist getting in the last word.

The meeting broke up, everyone filing from the office.

The last to follow, Bishop closed the door. The group ahead of him were less than enthusiastic about Stone having been placed over Bishop.

"Eddie, it sucks," Jack O'Leary said. He turned to look at Bishop. "You been running things around here awhile now. Bringing Stone in like that is a kick in the balls."

"Don't sweat it, Jack," Bishop said. "The senator is the man. He pays the bills, so he gets to choose."

"I know you, Jack. You're as pissed as we are."

"But right now I have to suck it up. No choice." Bishop smiled. "Game isn't over yet, just don't you forget that." He slapped O'Leary on his broad shoulder. "Don't ever forget it."

Bishop took out his cell and called Captain Fitch. The cop's phone went on to the message service. The same thing happened when Bishop tried Brenner and Dunn. Neither of them were on line. He tried a couple of more times then gave up. He'd left messages. He couldn't do anything more, and had his own business to handle anyhow. Let the cops deal with Stone. Maybe he could get them off their collective ass.

8

Henry Fitch, Captain, Seattle PD, was the first to arrive. He parked his unmarked car and sat studying the deserted building. Rain marked the windshield, blurring the image. He was at a loss to understand why Senator Kendal had called this meeting at such a location. He knew that Kendal had a thing about secrecy, not wanting to be seen with too many people outside his close group, but this was extreme. Fitch wasn't going to make too many waves. He was deep in with Kendal, taking his money and enjoying the privileges the man was able to bestow. So if Kendal called a meeting to discuss something important, Fitch had no real choice. He glanced again at his watch. At least he was on time. That was always important where Kendal was concerned. The senator had a thing about punctuality. It was one of his rules—and it didn't do to break any of his rules. Fitch consoled himself by thinking about the bank accounts where he had his money squirreled away. Police pensions were one thing—Senator Kendal's payoffs were another.

A car nosed into view between a couple of the deserted buildings, splashing its way across to pull up alongside Fitch's. Despite the spattering of rain on the window, Fitch recognized Detective Steve Dunn as the man got out of the car, pulling on a waterproof coat. Dunn raised a quick hand. On the other side of the car Dunn's partner, Ken Brenner, stepped out the passenger door. Dunn pointed at the building's side door, then he and Brenner headed for it. Fitch dragged his own waterproof jacket from the rear seat and pulled it on. He shoved open his door and stepped out. Rain hit him with a cold hand and he legged it for the open side door.

Inside the building it was cold and dusty, shadows marking the floor. What light there was came from semi-transparent roof panels.

"How come you didn't tell us you were coming, too?" Dunn said. He was shaking the collar of his coat, shedding rain.

"Because I didn't know you were. Kendal's text just said time and place."

"That's what ours said," Brenner acknowledged.

Dunn said, "Must be important if he set up a meet this way." He always stated the obvious.

"You don't say," Fitch said.

"Maybe something happened about Logan," Brenner said.

"He wouldn't want to broadcast that," Dunn said.

"At least we're on time," Fitch said. "Jesus, it's cold in here."

"No heating on," Dunn said.

Fitch stared at him. "He ever come up with anything startling?" he asked Brenner.

"No. Ken likes to keep things on level ground."

Dunn said, "You talking about me?"

"Yes, I am, partner."

"Well, don't…"

Fitch raised a hand. "You hear that?" He reached inside his coat for his handgun.

"Not a wise move, Fitch."

The voice came from their left, from deep shadow. A tall figure detached from the dark and stepped into light. Dressed in black street clothes, the man stood over six feet, with thick black hair framing a strong-boned face, and blue eyes that were fixed on the three cops.

The man held a big handgun that was easily recognizable

as a .357 Magnum Desert Eagle. A serious weapon in any cop's book—not to be ignored.

"All of you. Take out the guns and drop them on the floor. Use your left hands. I'm only saying it once. Choice is yours."

Fitch, Dunn and Brenner exchanged glances, hopes swiftly dashed because the big man had them dead to rights. There was no way any of them could draw and fire while he had the .357 on them. The auto pistols were eased from holsters and dropped to the floor.

"Kick them in my direction," Bolan said. He watched them comply.

"You know who we are?" Fitch said. "Cops."

"Correction," Bolan said. "Dirty cops. On Senator Kendal's payroll."

"Who the fuck says so?" Dunn said.

"Ray Logan."

"That snitch," Dunn said. "What does he know?"

"Enough to put you three behind bars for a long time."

"If he stays alive long enough."

Fitch punched Dunn on the arm. "Shut the fuck up, Steve." He turned back to Bolan. "You really believe you can buck Kendal? Do you have any idea what he has behind him?"

Bolan allowed himself a thin smile. "Hired muscle. Backup from Maxim Koretski. Less you three."

"You got nothing on us," Brenner said.

"I have Logan's evidence—photographs, tapes, documented data. That's why you've been desperate to find him. So you can destroy what he's gathered. And let's not forget the bank accounts you jokers have been using to stash the money Kendal's been paying you."

"Son of a fucking bitch," Dunn screamed, losing control and rushing Bolan.

The Executioner waited for the right moment as the cop came toward him. He might have had a non-termination policy as far as police officers were concerned, but it didn't stretch as far as lesser punishment when he was faced with dirty cops. Bolan let Dunn get to within a few feet, then swung the heavy Desert Eagle around in a wide arc that terminated against Dunn's left cheek and upper jaw. The steel bulk of the pistol landed with a meaty crunch and Dunn went down on the floor, bouncing against the filthy concrete. He twisted over on his side, blood pouring from the raw gash in his flesh.

The Desert Eagle was back on Fitch and Brenner before either of them could react. "Have I made my point?" Bolan said.

Fitch was having difficulty holding himself back. The unwavering muzzle of the Desert Eagle persuaded him it might be advisable. "Okay, okay," he said. "So what happens now?"

Bolan pointed at an upended steel cabinet. "Everything in your pockets on there. And I mean everything. Including any backup weapons. And one of you do it for him," he added, nodding in Dunn's direction.

Bolan stepped well back and watched as the two cops turned out their pockets and placed the items on the cabinet.

"You going to steal our money, too?" Brenner said.

"Why would I need to do that when I can clear your bank accounts? Believe me, I have friends who can do that without even breaking into a sweat."

"He's just trying to rile you," Fitch said.

Bolan instructed Brenner to collect the keys for the cars outside and also those for the sets of handcuffs, then he dropped them into one of his pockets.

"Get your pal on his feet," Bolan said. "Move to that steel pillar and cuff yourselves together. Wrists to wrists. You know the drill."

"This won't be forgotten, son of a bitch," Fitch said. "I'll have the whole of Seattle PD on your fuckin' tail."

Bolan waited until the three were secured, then unloaded the weapons laid out on the cabinet. He stripped the pistols into their component parts, scattering them across the building.

"Nice backup guns," he commented. "All unregistered? Of course they are. I'll take the cell phones. Might be able to pull something interesting off the call registers. Unless you guys cleared everything?"

The looks on their faces told him they most likely hadn't.

"I'm sure most of the cops in your precinct will be interested to find out what you fine officers have been up to. If there are any more on Kendal's payroll I think we'll be finding out soon enough."

"Let us out of here," Fitch yelled. His anger spilled over into almost incoherent rage as he began to scream and rant at Bolan. "You can't do this. We're cops, damn it. Cops."

"I already corrected you on that," Bolan said. "Dirty cops. The worst kind. If you were anything else you'd be dead by now. I've never fired on a cop, ever, clean or dirty. I won't start now. But you're not getting away from this. A call from a high up Fed to IA will start the ball rolling. After that..."

Bolan walked out of the building, collar up against the downpour and returned to where he had concealed his SUV. Once inside, door closed against the weather, he checked out the three cell phones he had acquired. He ran through the call lists on each one, checking them against each other until he isolated a single number they all had in common.

Bolan stared out through the windshield as he called the number on one of the phones. It rang out for a long time before someone picked up.

"Yeah?"

"Fitch, Dunn and Brenner—they've been talking to me. A lot. All about Kendal. Spilling their guts about how you people want to shut Ray Logan up. I was surprised how much they were willing to give away just to save themselves."

"Who the hell are you?"

"Let's say I have a vested interest in you people. All the way up to Senator Kendal's greasy neck. Word you can pass along to him is his day is coming. Soon. You're all on my wish list. And if you want to discuss matters with Fitch and Dunn and Brenner, you'll find them waiting for you."

Bolan gave details of the location where he had left the trio of cops, then hung up. He fired up the SUV, turned it around and drove away from the derelict site. He had completed what he needed to do here. Whatever happened to the three cops was out of his hands. The severity of any punishment would depend on who came looking for them. As he hadn't spoken to anyone from Seattle PD, and had only informed Kendal's people, the options were thin on the ground.

It was time to move on to the next phase of his operation.

9

"Being undercover didn't mean I've lost contact with everyone," Logan said. "I made a few discreet calls. One of my sources just told me about Marty Keegan. He was found dead in his apartment this morning by his cleaning woman. He'd been tethered to his bed and tortured. *Butchered* was how it was described to me. At the end, his throat had been cut through to the bone. Cooper, he was my link to Rachel and Tommy. He knew where they were hiding because he chose the place. We agreed I shouldn't know where until it was time for Rachel to come in. Now Marty's dead and I have no idea where my wife and son are."

Bolan had to strain to catch all Logan's words over the phone. His voice was still weak.

"We'll figure this out, Ray."

"Don't you understand, Cooper, it's *my* damn fault. I sent them away and I can't do a thing to help them. Kendal has all the cards..."

Logan's voice faded and all Bolan could hear was his labored breathing. His energy levels were way down and the pressure of not knowing where his wife and son were was taking its toll.

"I had a talk with your cop buddies—Fitch, Dunn and Brenner. They didn't send their best wishes. I think it's safe to say they won't be bothering you anymore."

"They aren't going to just sit around, Cooper."

"When I left, they were kind of tied up."

"Couldn't happen to a nicer bunch of guys."

"Ray, I'm going to call someone who might be able to pin down where Rachel is. You take it easy and we'll talk soon."

Bolan broke the connection, immediately hitting the speed dial for Stony Man Farm. He needed to speak to his main source of help—the cyber chief, Kurtzman. When Kurtzman came on, the urgency in Bolan's tone warned him there was no time for the usual banter.

"A Seattle cop," Bolan said. "Marty Keegan. Murdered today. Run a deep background check on him, Bear. I think he was killed for information on the wife and son of another cop, the one I'm helping out. Keegan had relocated Logan's wife and kid to a safe place outside the city. He was the only one who knew the hideout location. I need to find them. I'll explain later. Go into everything about Keegan. And I need it fast."

"Sounds urgent, Striker."

"Lives may depend on it."

Bolan heard Kurtzman giving instructions to his cyber team. He knew they would be dropping everything to move into action.

Akira Tokaido.

Huntington "Hunt" Wethers.

Carmen Delahunt.

The most accomplished computer team ever assembled existed at the Stony Man Farm, equipped with the best electronic equipment money could buy. They were led by Kurtzman, wheelchair-bound maybe, but not held back by this physical disability. The big bear of a man had yet to come across a code he couldn't crack or a firewall he couldn't douse. If the late Marty Keegan had secrets, Kurtzman and his team would find them.

Kurtzman's call came back after an hour.

"We ran an in-depth, extensive profile on the man. Family history, his personal data. And I think we may have found what you're looking for. No guarantees, Striker, but I have a feeling we hit pay dirt."

"I guessed you would."

"Keegan's family is native to the area. He's Seattle-born and -bred. Been a cop all his adult life. We tracked him through every document available, including bank statements, and tied together the fact that he pays annual property insurance on a cabin way up in the Cascades. It was willed to him by his deceased grandfather. Pretty remote, beside a small lake, no utilities, so we checked and found he paid by check for fuel deliveries through a local supplier. I'm guessing for a diesel generator to provide power. Your cop has a secluded cabin. Off the track, that no one seems to know about."

"Worth checking out," Bolan said. "Can you give me a GPS location?"

"I'll download it. Striker, if this is what you wanted and Keegan was killed most likely for the same thing…"

"Just what I'm thinking," Bolan said. "What's your time estimate?"

"Three hours. You hit the road now you should make it by midday."

"Let's hope the opposition isn't so sharp on the uptake."

"Coordinates downloading now."

Bolan checked the downloaded information. "Got it. Thanks, Bear."

"Good hunting, Striker."

Bolan was already rolling. He had tapped in the coordinates and the soothing voice on the satnav was already instructing him which route would get him out of the city and on the road north.

10

"I love America," Maxim Koretski said.

"You love American dollars," Senator Tyrone Kendal corrected.

"Yes, that, too. But I like the ambition here. The striving for a better life. The truth that greed *is* good."

"Jesus, Max, that's just a line from a goddamn movie."

"Perhaps. But it is a wonderful line. I like the sentiment."

"Let's cut the crap, Max. You fucked up, *tovarich*. Sending your people to Ray Logan's house was a clumsy move."

"I sent them to search for the evidence that cop has gathered. It had to be done. I am involved in this as much as you are."

"No one disputes that, Max, but why didn't you consult me first? I could have told you my people had already checked out the place. They found nothing, as we suspected. Logan's no fool. He wouldn't leave his evidence lying around in his own home."

"I was trying to help. And I need to protect myself, as well."

"Of course you do. But, Max, it went wrong and both your men ended up dead. Two dead Russians. I'm damn sure Logan has heard about that. People could start asking awkward questions. Look, we're getting close here. Too close to success to screw things up. We need to suppress Logan's information, but we can't risk too many confrontations where people might start asking questions. So before you do anything talk it over with me. We should work as a team."

Koretski shrugged. As powerful as he was, the Russian often displayed a naive manner. He considered himself untouchable. His Russian nature cloaked him in a reckless attitude. He was direct almost to the point of arrogance. If he didn't need the man, Kendal might have had Stone cut his throat and be done with it. But until that moment arrived, the American tolerated his bullish partner.

Kendal sensed another question on its way. The Russian leaned forward, his eyes fixing on the senator.

"So who killed my men?" he asked. "Earlier you said it had nothing to do with the police."

"I had it checked out. There was no police involvement, nor anything from the FBI, or Homeland Security. We followed this all down the line. Logically speaking, there was no reason anyone should have been on the spot when your team went into Logan's house."

"So who are we talking about? This third party, who is he? Where does he come from?"

"I have a theory, Max. The only other individual on the scene no one seems to have considered. Or mentioned."

"Yes?"

"The man in the SUV who showed up and pulled Logan off the street while he was evading Fitch's two officers. The one who fired on Dunn and Brenner. We have to assume he's thrown in with Logan—for whatever reason."

"Why would he do that? It makes no sense. Unless he knows Logan."

"The way Fitch heard it from Dunn and Brenner, this man showed up out of the blue. He could not have known Logan would run from that alley at that precise moment. There was no prearranged rendezvous."

"We need to look into this. If Logan has some kind of accomplice it could cause us more problems."

"I agree. I'll put someone on it. More important, we still need to locate Logan and his wife."

"So, have your people come any closer to finding them?"

Kendal smiled, enjoying the moment.

"I have a team on their way right now to detain Rachel and Tommy Logan," he said. "My specialist got the information from Logan's police partner. It appears he had assisted in helping Logan's wife disappear and only he knew where she is."

"I congratulate you, Tyrone. Your man must be extremely persuasive."

"He is. He has a unique way of asking questions that never fails."

"And Logan's partner?"

"Ex-partner," Kendal said. "My man saw to that."

Koretski nodded. "A good, clean result. No loose ends left behind. I like that, too." Koretski asked, "What about Logan's evidence?"

"When we get our hands on the wife I'm sure things will sort themselves out. Either Logan has it, or his wife hid it somewhere out of reach. Once we have them all together someone will be made to talk."

"Your *specialist?*"

"He will get us what we want."

"I would like to meet this man," Koretski said. "He sounds exceptional."

"He is not a social animal," Kendal said. "He prefers his own company. But if the occasion arises I will introduce you."

Koretski pushed to his feet. "As much as *I* enjoy *your* company, Tyrone, I think it is time for me to leave. There's much to do."

"The helicopter is waiting for you." Kendal stood and shook the Russian's hand. "I will keep you informed. Stay in touch. In a few days we will be ready to go. By then I'm confident the Logan affair will be over."

"I hope so," Koretski said. "It has gone on for long enough."

11

Bolan braked and brought the SUV to a stop. He cut the motor and sat studying the small huddle of timber buildings ahead. On his drive up from the city he had checked in with Kurtzman again to gain intel on the area. Stony Man Farm had come up with the name and location of the general store and gas station that served the local area. There were a few other cabins dotted around the store. The cabin belonging to the late Marty Keegan was higher up the trail, near an isolated lake, close on five miles from where Bolan currently sat. He noticed the rough, partly overgrown trail winding its way toward the higher elevation.

The first thing Bolan spotted was the late-model, gleaming SUV parked up close to the general store. Next to it was a less glamorous Ford truck, its paintwork faded and showing the marks of being driven constantly through the heavy foliage that lined the approach road and the trails out. That vehicle fitted the scene. The brand-new SUV did not.

Bolan picked up on the silence. There was smoke coming from the chimney of the store but no sign of any movement. He stepped out of his SUV, checked the Beretta holstered beneath his jacket and made his way toward the store. He made his approach so that he passed the post window before he reached the door. The interior appeared deserted. Then he caught movement inside as someone moved to one side of the door.

Bolan reached the door, pushed the handle and let the door swing wide. He stepped inside.

He looked beyond the stacked goods, the chiller unit and the shelves. The counter faced him and behind it stood a middle-aged woman dressed in a checkered shirt. The smile on her face was as rigid as a painted doll's as she stared at Bolan. To his right he sensed a motionless figure and a shadow on the wood floor. The outline of the shadow showed an arm and a hand holding a gun.

The shadow moved as the gunman stepped away from the inside wall, the weapon in his hand moving to cover Bolan.

Bolan turned, his left hand sweeping round, fingers clamping over the barrel of the auto pistol. He yanked the surprised gunman forward, off balance, and as the startled man slid into view Bolan struck out with his bunched right fist. It caught the guy in the jaw, bone crunching under the force of the blow. Bolan yanked the pistol from the man's hand, then used it to hit him across the other side of his face. A bloody gash opened in his cheek as he was slammed back against the wall. Before the thug could recover, Bolan used the butt of the auto pistol on the back of his skull. The guy went down without a sound.

"You hurt?" Bolan asked the woman.

She shook her head. "But my husband…they beat him…"

"You go tend to him," Bolan said.

A quick search of the store and Bolan found some plastic ties. He secured the unconscious gunman's ankles and wrists, then crossed the store to assist the woman. She was on her knees beside the bloodied figure of her husband. He had been beaten around the face and head. Bolan checked his pulse. It was steady and the wounds were not deep enough to be life-threatening. Bolan lifted him into one of the wooden chairs set near the counter while the woman went to get the first-aid box.

"How many others were there?" Bolan asked.

"Three. They made Arthur give them directions to Marty Keegan's place. That one stayed behind to make sure we didn't contact anyone." She stared across at Bolan. "You come to help that young woman and her boy? She's all alone up there."

"That's the general idea."

"I hope you get there in time."

"How are those three getting up there?"

The woman said, "They went in their 4x4 less than an hour ago. Arthur didn't tell them they won't get all the way like that. They'll get themselves lost, too, if they're not careful. Damned city boys by the look of them. Not used to walking in the woods. Now that trail peters out well before the cabin. More than likely they'll have to abandon it and go on foot."

"Is there a faster route?"

"Yes. Go behind the store, head due north until you hit the ridge. Can't miss it. Then cut toward the west. Keep the peaks ahead of you. A mile and you'll be on high ground. The lake where Marty's cabin sits will be in view. That way you're cutting off more than half the distance."

"That'll be handy."

"One thing. Those three put on some kind of headsets just before they left. They were checking them. Does that mean anything?"

It did. Comsets.

"Lets them talk to each other if they get separated."

"You think they might? Get separated I mean."

Bolan smiled. "If I have anything to do with it."

"Make sure you do."

"You going to be okay now?"

She nodded. Touched Bolan's arm. "You get up to that woman and her boy. We'll be fine now. I'll see to Arthur then fetch his Winchester off the pegs. That son of a bitch isn't going to be any bother." She stared at Bolan for a moment. "You some kind of lawman?"

"You could say that, ma'am."

"Nobody's called me 'ma'am' in years," she said, smiling. "Like having John Wayne back. Now you get out of here quick." She put out a hand to touch his arm. "Should I call the police?"

"Be grateful if you didn't. Right now they could be a problem if you do. Do you trust me, ma'am?"

"Yes."

"Just keep that guy tied up. If he tries to persuade you to set him free play deaf."

"After what they did to Arthur he's lucky I haven't already turned that 44-40 on him. And by the way, my name is Sarah."

"Matt Cooper. Just keep your eyes and ears open, Sarah."

"You think there might be more coming?"

"Maybe."

Sarah recognized the concern in his eyes. "You get moving, son. Worry about that young woman and her boy. This time I'm more than ready if any of those town bullies show up. We got the Winchester and a couple of handguns. Even got a pump-action 12-gauge in back. And my Arthur was a Marine way back. Gunnery sergeant, too. Now go. Bring that pair out safe."

"Anyone else around who might help you?"

"Only me and Arthur here this time of year. All the other cabins are closed up."

Bolan made his way back to the SUV. He opened the rear door and unzipped his weapons bag. He shed his civilian clothing and geared up in camo suit and boots, Beretta and MP-5, filling the pouches of his combat harness with extra magazines. He also slid his Cold Steel Tanto into its belt sheath. He was satisfied that the ordnance he carried would serve for what he had to do. Time was short on this phase, so he didn't want to burden himself with too much equipment.

He circled the trading post and pushed into the dense forest, following the directions he had been given.

Silence surrounded him, save for the natural sounds of birds and wildlife in the deep undergrowth. The forest engulfed him. Trees and bush grew in thick abundance. Bolan held his MP-5 close to his chest as he moved along a barely visible trail. He kept the distant ridge directly ahead, aware that the terrain was rising gradually. Not a harsh climb. A natural swell in the ground underfoot. Bolan felt, if not entirely at home, at least comfortable in this environment. In times past he had undergone similar treks, often in surroundings that were totally hostile. Not just in regard to wildlife, but with vegetation that could scratch and tear at flesh. This forest, dense as it was, held no discernable threats except for the men he was tracking.

Bolan never found himself at odds with the environment, but man was a different element. He could be violent and untrustworthy. Exhibiting traits that even so-called wild animals would never show. Animals responded to threats against their lives and territory, whereas man had the capacity to be both duplicitous and cruel. Bolan could understand the need to defend and protect. That was the forte of animals in their natural world. Man brought his own brand of viciousness with him—the need to dominate, to inflict suffering and terror on his fellow man. Greed and selfishness were man's domain.

Those characteristics, and more, were part of the reason why the Executioner existed. His fight against the evil in man, something that had always manifested itself, continued and would remain as long as the conditions demanded. At this time in his life Bolan saw little chance of that changing. So he moved on, facing the challenge, and accepted it without complaint.

Bolan moved at a steady, distance-eating pace. He understood the urgency of the moment, but chose to hold himself back from any headlong rush. Exhausting himself before reaching any confrontation was foolish. He needed both stamina and containment, so that when he did confront his enemy, his physical and mental limits were at their best.

Before he reached the crest of the ridge, tracking toward the west, the way became denser, the timber and foliage closing in so that he had to physically force his way through. If this was how his quarry was finding travel, he could understand why it would be difficult for a land-based vehicle to penetrate.

He broke free of the undergrowth and saw the distant peaks ahead of him. An endless spread of forest layered the slopes. Bolan moved off again. He covered the mile distance with ease, noticing he was moving upward again, and the sun glinting on the lake ahead brought him to a cautious stop, crouching as he surveyed the terrain in front of him. Following the edge of the lake, scanning the area, Bolan made out the shape of the cabin. He fixed the position of the structure before pushing on, checking back in the direction the approaching team would be coming from.

The men searching for Ray Logan's wife and son would have no charitable thoughts where they were concerned. Bolan had seen the results of their attitude in the beaten store owner. He recalled Logan's description of Keegan's death.

Okay, they had already drawn the parameters.

So the Executioner would base his delivery along those lines.

12

The trio Vigo Stone had sent to bring in Logan's family were already out of their comfort zone. The first setback had been losing the SUV. They were still some distance from the cabin when the dense forest became almost impossible to drive through. And then Madden, taking the wheel after they left Lohman at the store, had gotten the vehicle wedged between a pair of massive trees. The more he sat on the gas, the tighter the SUV had gotten stuck.

"Jake, switch the fuckin' motor off," Rubin said. "We ain't going any farther in this thing. They'll have to cut the damn trees down to get it free."

Madden cut the power and slammed his fists against the steering wheel in frustration. "Crap piece of garbage," he said.

Behind him Burdett laughed. "Crap driving more like," he said. "And quit pounding the wheel. You want to set off the airbag?"

"Why didn't that son of a bitch back at the store tell us we couldn't ride all the way up?" Madden said.

"We aren't exactly on his friendly list, that's why," Burdett said. "You did walk all over his face."

Rubin pulled the sat phone from his pocket and keyed in a number. "Yeah, it's me. You got that cabin on your GPS? So get that chopper hell up here. We're having to go the rest of the way on foot. The freakin' car can't get any farther. It's stuck.... What do you expect me to do? Go at the friggin' trees with a machete?... No, it isn't possible... Stone ain't going to like it? Well, tough shit. Send him along and let's see if he can do any better. Just hang back until I give you the word. I don't want that woman hearing the helicopter until we got her contained." He threw the phone down and snatched up his SMG. "Let's go. Time to hit the fuckin' nature trail."

As they exited the vehicle and pushed forward on foot, Madden said, "We get back down to that freakin' store I'm going to skin that storekeeper." He struggled through the heavy foliage. "I hate the forest."

They pushed on as fast as they were able.

"You know what I'm thinking," Burdett said.

"What?"

"We should just shoot the bitch and her brat and be done with it."

Rubin shook his head. "Want to know what I think?"

"What?"

"You should shut the fuck up. Now let's spread out so we can cover more of the cabin in case the Logan woman has company. You guys left and right. I'll keep the middle path. Stay in touch through the comsets."

BOLAN'S PATH OF TRAVEL brought him in line with the incoming team. He moved with consummate ease through the foliage, using the light and shadow for cover, and he saw them long before they knew he was around.

He also heard them. The sound of their passing. The inane chatter over the comsets they wore for communication, though with the nonstop jawing the last thing they needed were electronic devices to transmit.

He gave them credit for getting close, but it was not good enough. The sound they created transmitted itself to the concealed soldier. Bolan had honed his craft in countless missions in all parts of the world. He recognized natural sounds and picked out those made by invaders to the forested terrain—small fragments of sound that did not belong. And it was the intrusion of those sound bites that provided him with the markers that betrayed the newcomers.

These men were far from their natural habitat. The woman at the store had judged them correctly. They belonged in the urban streets, not in a forested world that closed around them and amplified every move they made. And they talked incessantly over the digital comsets they wore. That chatter, slight as it was, still reached Bolan's ears. He even heard *Logan* and *Rachel*. These men talked too much. It pinpointed them as targets clearer than a flashing beacon. Bolan established the relative positions of the three men and let them pass before he eased out of concealment, closing on the nearest guy, getting his first physical view of the opposition.

Their participation in the hunt for Rachel Logan tied them into the death of Marty Keegan. They, or someone within their group, had tortured him to death for information. Logan's loyal friend had suffered at the hands of these people simply because he knew the runaway cop and would not give up on him. They were guns for hire. Eager to prove their skills to the man who paid them. At this moment they were looking for Rachel Logan and her son, and Bolan had no doubts as to the kind of treatment they would mete out if they got their hands on the woman and the boy.

Bolan slung the MP-5 from his shoulder and unholstered his handgun. He raised the Beretta and tracked in on his first target.

The guy never knew what hit him. The 93-R coughed three times. The subsonic 9 mm Parabellum slugs took his skull apart and briefly misted the air with bloody debris as bone and flesh and brain fragments parted from the shattered head. The man went down with nothing more than a muffled grunt, his body slack and heavy. He struck the forest floor facedown, dying nerves making him shudder for a few seconds before all movement ceased.

His partners must have heard the man's dying grunt through their comsets. As one, they came to a stop, weapons circling the area. They realized something had happened.

Bolan was already angling in through the undergrowth, his auto pistol held forward as he closed the gap. He moved a few yards to his left, having identified a dark-clad figure clutching a squat SMG directly ahead.

The guy made eye contact, face taut with the reality of being confronted by a figure who seemed to have magically emerged from the greenery. As Bolan's form took shape the man brought his SMG round, the muzzle traversing to align on this newcomer.

The 93-R spat out a second triburst and the guy's body jerked under the impact of the 9 mm slugs coring through his chest. They shattered bone and cleaved their way into his pumping heart. He stumbled back, arms flailing as he tried, without success, to stay upright. He slammed to the ground on his back, the impact causing a spraying gout of blood to erupt from his open mouth. His weapon flew from his slack fingers. The man convulsed, coughing up more blood as his punctured heart gave out.

RUBIN DROPPED TO A CROUCH. He was close enough to have seen his buddy go down. He drew himself tight, peering through the tangle of green, and tried to pick out the shooter. He quickly became aware he was out of his depth. This place was alien to him—a mass of tangled greenery, tall trees with a canopy of intertwining branches and leaves that almost shut out the sky. The silence all around him was unnerving. The only sound was his own ragged breathing. Back in the city he might have been a tough guy, but here he was a total novice.

Something crackled close by, to his right. Rubin loosed off a short burst from his SMG. The sound was loud in the forest. He jerked as birds erupted from the shrubbery. They flew about in erratic motion. One swooped down and swerved violently in front of his face. He slapped at it with his left hand, involuntarily half-rising from his crouch.

And that was when he saw the shooter. Only yards away, standing in front of him. The guy had a grim expression on his face and he fixed him with eyes as cold as a bleak winter sky.

There was a big handgun in the man's large fist. Rubin didn't recognize the weapon's configuration—not that it mattered. It was the last thing he saw before the Beretta fired and three 9 mm slugs took his face apart in a blinding flash. He dropped to the ground, numb from the impact, so he didn't see Bolan move the 93-R's selector to single shot, stand over him and trigger a final shot that seared into his brain and brought on the final darkness.

BOLAN CROSSED TO WHERE the second guy lay, taking short, labored breaths. His single tap shut the guy down.

None of the three carried any ID. No personal items. Only one carried a phone. A sat phone. Bolan tucked it in a side pocket for later inspection. Each man had a holstered auto pistol and they had all carried SMGs. Bolan took all the arms and stowed them inside a long-fallen, rotting log, scooping leaves over the open end. Then he moved on, the Beretta back in its holster, the MP-5 taken from his shoulder and brought into play.

Bolan didn't expect any further distractions at this moment in time. It would have been expected that three armed men would be sufficient to track through the forest to deal with a single woman and a young boy. They hadn't counted Bolan into the equation, but then a trio of experienced shooters should have been a large enough force to handle him.

One against three.

The odds in their favor.

Their mistake.

They didn't understand a man like Bolan. A seasoned soldier who had operated in every combat situation ever conceived. Who walked the hellgrounds with the ease that any other man might walk his city streets. The ultimate soldier. A man who had learned his craft in military conflicts, then moved on to initiate his *own* war. Bolan's personal war was directed toward the eradication of Evil in all its forms. It had taken on a life of its own. Bolan against Animal Man. Dedicated to removing the defilers of decency, and those who perpetrated insane horrors against their own. Bolan sought them out and delivered the just verdict that was sufficient to end their crimes.

Their execution? Final payment for what they had done, were still doing. And for as long as he was able, Bolan would continue his war.

As he would on this day.

As always.

As it had to be.

13

Bolan came up on the cabin minutes later, pausing to assess the layout before he moved in quickly and silently. He flattened against the front wall, back pressed to the rough timber. He heard nothing from inside. When he moved it was swiftly, his approach direct, because he had a feeling there might be others ready to back up the three he had taken down. He hadn't seen or heard any other intruders, but Bolan never took anything for granted. Letting his guard down was an invitation for disaster.

He stepped up onto the porch, reached the door, and pushed against the handle. The door swung inward on creaking hinges and Bolan went in fast and low, his raised MP-5 sweeping the interior, picking up the two figures just off center from the door.

Bolan came face-to-face with Rachel Logan.

Even in her disheveled state she was a strikingly beautiful woman. Her creased shirt and faded jeans did nothing to take away from her looks. Thick, tawny-blond hair, in need of a good brushing, framed her face, and the hard stare she gave Bolan was emphasized by the steely expression in her green-flecked eyes. The ten-year-old boy at her side, a miniature Ray Logan, held his own defiant look.

"You take one more step I'll shoot," she said. The Colt Commander in her right hand was aimed at Bolan's chest and the barrel was rock-steady. "Believe it."

"Ray told me you mean what you say." Bolan lowered the

MP-5, held his hands clear from his body and kept his voice neutral, his expression benign.

Rachel backed off, her eyes searching his face for any signs of deceit. "Is this where you convince me Ray sent you? That I should trust you? Do I look that stupid?"

"I'm not going to say that with a gun pointed at me. Rachel, I know the trouble Ray is in. We met while he was on the run from two cops on Senator Kendal's payroll. I managed to get him clear and into cover. Since then I've been chased by Kendal's hired guns and Russian shooters and managed to keep one step ahead. Right now I have Ray in a safe house so he can start to recover…"

"*Recover?* From what?"

"He took a couple of bullets the night we ran into each other. The bullets have been removed and he's resting. He's weak but he'll be fine. My concern is you and the boy."

"My name is Tommy, not *boy*," the youngster said.

Bolan smiled. "I know, Tommy."

"How do I know you're telling the truth?" Rachel said. "This could all be a trick."

"It could, but it isn't."

Bolan let the MP-5 hang from its sling, took his sat phone from a pocket and hit the speed dial for Logan's burn phone. He waited until the call was answered.

"Ray, I have someone who wants to talk to you," Bolan said and handed the phone to Rachel.

She took it and listened, her face crumpling after a few seconds, tears pooling in her eyes.

"Yes. We're okay. In a mess, but okay. This man just showed up, he says he knows you… Ray, he said you got shot." She listened as Logan spoke. "All right, love. Don't worry, we'll get through this." She handed the phone back to Bolan. "He needs to speak to you."

"Cooper, what do I say? You found them."

"I had to go through three of Kendal's hit squad to get to them. They were already close to reaching them. Too close. And I'm guessing there may be others around."

"You have to get them clear, Cooper. Before Kendal's shooters show up."

"I'll handle it, Ray. Now I need to get Rachel and your son away from here. I'll let you know where when we talk next time."

"I'll trash this phone when we're done. I have another with me. I'll use it when I make contact next time, so you won't know the number until I do."

"Good idea. You need to talk to Rachel again?"

Bolan handed the phone back to Rachel, then crossed to look out the window, studying the lay of the land. The thick stands of timber and the tangled undergrowth made spotting movement difficult. Bolan's knowledge of any more intruders was practically nil at that moment. If any more of Kendal's hired guns were close to the cabin they had the advantage for the time being. So the sooner he and Logan's family moved out, the better their chances.

Rachel handed him the phone. Bolan stowed it in his pocket. She sent Tommy to pack their gear, giving her a moment with Bolan.

"Ray said I should trust you. He told me how you stepped in and helped. Thank you, Mr. Cooper."

"It's Matt. Your husband is a brave man to stand up to these people."

"I know that," Rachel said. "And stubborn. Matt, I heard you had to come through Kendal's people. Do I take that to mean what I think it does?"

Bolan nodded. "They're set on silencing Ray and getting the information he has. They will do anything to achieve that. The only way to stop them is to…"

"Is to do it to them first. I might not have agreed a short time back," she said, "but I see your point."

Bolan indicated the Colt she still held in her left hand. The gun was hanging loose at her side.

"Can you shoot with that?"

"I'm proficient," she said. "Only at targets, though. Never shot at a human being."

"Difference is a man moves and, more importantly, he can shoot back," Bolan said. "If it comes to the crunch don't hesitate. You won't get a second shot. Aim for the body. Biggest target."

"I understand. Mr.…*Matt*…where do we go?"

"Until Ray's evidence is handed in you're all under threat. My priority is to get you out of here and to a safe place."

"I thought we were safe here," Rachel said. "No one was supposed to know where we were. Only Marty. He wouldn't tell anyone where we were. Not even Ray. We decided if Ray didn't know…" She stopped then, her gaze fixed on Bolan. He knew what was coming even before she sensed his awareness. "God, no. Not Marty. Tell me, Cooper. Did they get to Marty and make him talk?"

Bolan saw that Tommy was staring at him, as well. The boy's eyes were wide, filled with anticipation of bad news.

"Did they hurt Uncle Marty?" he asked. "Did they?"

"Sorry, son." Bolan took a step forward. "He was a brave man. But they made him tell."

Tommy raised his head, tears glistening in his eyes. "Don't lie to me," he said. "Is he dead?"

The words threatened to choke in Bolan's throat. "Yes, Tommy" was all he could say.

The boy clung to his mother's side, turning his face to her. Rachel, fighting back her own grief, looked at Bolan. She understood his reluctance at having to tell it as it was, but the news of Keegan's death was not something Bolan could have denied either of them.

"Now you understand the kind of people we're up against," Bolan said as gently as he could. "Which is why we can't give in to them. For Marty's sake and for Ray."

Rachel cleared her throat, head up. She said, "That's something we won't do, Matt. Believe me. We won't."

"Do you have everything you need?" Bolan asked.

Rachel pulled on a faded denim jacket and tucked her Colt into her jeans. "That's it. We're ready."

"I take it you know the area?"

"Pretty much."

"My vehicle is parked at the store. If they have more men in the vicinity, we can't go directly to it. We need to circle round. Come in from a different direction so I can check the situation."

Rachel nodded, understanding. "We can take the high ground and cut back through the valley that runs parallel to where we are. Be a good distance to cover and it'll be dark before we get back to the store."

"We can make the night work for us. Okay, Rachel you cut the trail. I'll bring up the rear. We move fast but don't take any chances. Last thing we need are any injuries that might slow us down. Just one more thing. If I tell you and Tommy to do something…"

"I know. Don't question why, just do it." Rachel grinned. "I understand the situation. This isn't a fun trek. It's serious."

Bolan opened the cabin door. "Let's go," he said.

14

Bolan was standing in the open doorway when he picked up the rising sound. It was one he was familiar with—an incoming helicopter. He moved to the door and scanned the treetops, spotting the blue-and-white configuration of the chopper as it came into sight.

"There a back door?"

"Yes," Rachel said, and they all moved to the rear of the cabin.

The thwack of the chopper's rotors told Bolan their time was almost up. They had to get out before Kendal's crew reached them and blocked any escape.

"Stay close to your mother, Tommy. When we get outside, you start running, and just keep it that way. Watch where you run, not around you. Don't take your eyes off the way ahead. Understand?"

The boy nodded.

"Just stay ahead of me," Bolan said to Rachel. "I'll watch your back. You'll be covered."

They reached the back door and Bolan pulled it open. There was a cleared area at the rear of the cabin, starting to grow back. Bolan figured it had been a fire break originally. Beyond it the trees grew close and heavy.

"Head for the trees," Bolan said. "They'll give cover but keep moving because once they see we're gone they'll come after us."

The rotor sound was getting louder.

"What about the evidence?" Rachel asked.

"Later. Right now I want you and Tommy clear and safe. Let me worry about the evidence. Now *go*."

Rachel and Tommy cleared the stoop and broke into a headlong run. Rachel had one of his hands in hers, but she needn't have worried. The boy's long-legged pace kept him up with her.

Bolan followed seconds later, his MP-5 in his hands, his eyes searching constantly.

The sound of the helicopter swelled and he knew, without looking back, that it was over the cabin. He turned around and saw it dropping on the far side. Disembarking some of its passengers. If they had any foresight they would circle the cabin and check the rear. If their skills were along the lines of the three Bolan had dealt with earlier, he suspected they might not follow through. It would give Bolan and Rachel a little more breathing space and allow them to push deeper into the timber.

If only.

Maybe.

Bolan wasn't going to let himself become complacent. They were being pursued by a larger force who had the chopper for additional backup. Bolan had no idea how large the ground team was. There was no easy way to get themselves clear away from pursuit, so Bolan was going to have to rely on his own combat experience to keep them ahead of their enemies. Clear in Bolan's mind was the fact that Rachel and Tommy were the prime targets of the ground force. They might not want them dead at this stage, but in the finale of any scenario, once Kendal had what he wanted, the woman and the boy would be superfluous to his requirements. Kendal was playing for high stakes, Bolan was sure. High enough for murder to be an acceptable act. The shooting of Ray Logan and the savage death of Marty Keegan proved that. Bolan wouldn't allow it to happen to Logan's wife and son.

Kendal and his crew had set the standard. Bolan would make certain they would have the same visited on them.

Ahead Rachel and the boy moved into the trees, the shadows pulling in around them.

Bolan heard a shout behind him and then the crackle of auto fire. Felt slugs slap the ground around him.

Game on.

He kept moving, increasing his pace, knowing that as long as he was in the open he presented a clear target. More auto fire. Slugs zipped into the grass, a couple even closer than the first volley.

And then he was surrounded by trees, the blessed trunks and low branches shielding him. Bolan heard shots slam into the timber, chewing bark and ripping at the foliage. He pulled up short, taking cover behind a thick tree trunk, and raised his SMG, waiting for the opposition to get in range. His move led them to believe he was still moving ahead. Bolan let them believe.

Overhead, the dark bulk of the hovering helicopter appeared, the rotor wash and the spinning blades dominating the scene. The men on the ground were waving it away, but the pilot, and whoever commanded the team from the cabin, ignored their pleas.

Bolan shouldered the MP-5, tracked the ground team and gave them a couple of short bursts—two went down, three others scattered. One of the downed men was clutching a torn shoulder, the effects of the 9 mm slugs taking away his desire to fight on. The other guy was on his stomach, motionless.

The chopper swung in toward the treeline, unable to get in too close. Bolan edged around to the far side of the tree, leaning against the trunk to steady his aim. He let go with a long burst, concentrating on the chopper's engine housing. The range was close enough for his slugs to have a damaging effect on the craft. The 9 mm rounds hammered at the aluminum panels, punching ragged holes in the metal. Bolan held his finger on the trigger and cleared the MP-5's magazine. The chopper's power faltered, the smooth beat becoming ragged. The pilot, realizing he had sustained damage, hauled back on the controls and the machine moved away from the treeline, starting to come down on the open ground behind the cabin.

Bolan ejected the empty mag, plucking a fresh one from his harness, working the slide to put a fresh round into the breech and swung the SMG back in the direction of the ground team. The first guy to respond came bulling in like he had a death wish, his own FN P90 crackling as he fired on the move. He had a fair fix on where Bolan was concealed and the slugs from his weapon chewed timber and shredded leaves only feet away from the soldier. Bolan admired his initiative, but it did nothing to lessen his response. The Executioner fired a steady burst that ripped into the advancing figure, cutting a bloody swathe of hurt to his midsection. The guy yelled, his SMG's muzzle drooping and his final volley pounding the ground at his feet. As he slumped to his knees Bolan put him down with a final burst to his upper chest.

Briefly held back by the sight of their buddy going down, the remaining two allowed Bolan to turn and move deeper into the forest. Bolan picked up the pace. In the middle distance he could see the figures of Rachel and Tommy. They had heeded his advice and were still moving fast, having ignored the rattle of gunfire. The advantage was still theirs, and they had to maintain it. But Bolan was aware it might not last. There were still the two survivors of the ground team, plus however many men had been in the helicopter. An unknown figure at the moment—but Bolan had a feeling it wouldn't be for long.

15

The chopper landed hard, the pilot immediately cutting all power, shutting off fuel lines. He was cursing nonstop, bemoaning the fact his helicopter had taken damage and threatening all kinds of recriminations if he was not reimbursed for what had happened. His chopper was how he earned his living, and even though he had few scruples as to the nature of any business, his devotion to his beloved aircraft was total. As he stepped from the cockpit he raised his arms in a futile gesture when he saw smoke curling from the engine compartment.

"That's all I need," he said. "My fuckin' chopper totaled."

Ralphie Sprague, put in charge of the chopper team by Stone, waited until the final three shooters emerged from the helicopter. He instructed them to go check on the casualties, then turned on the pilot.

"What is your problem?" he asked.

The pilot jerked a hand in the direction of the chopper where more smoke was showing.

"That's my problem. That bird is liable to go up in flames any minute. You know how much one of those things costs? I could be out of fuckin' business in the next hour. Plus, I've been shot at. Nobody said anything about that. All I was told was I had to ferry a few guys up into the back country. No mention of getting shot at."

Sprague stared at the man as if he had grown a second head. His mind was full of what had happened to his team, the last thing he needed was some sky jockey whining about his damn helicopter.

"Stan? Right?"

"Yeah."

"Right now, Stan, if you make one more remark about your flea-bitten fuckin' chopper *I* am going to shoot you where you stand." His words were delivered with enough venom that even Stan understood. He took one look at Sprague's livid face and backed off.

"We good, Ralphie?" It was one of his hitters.

Sprague glanced at the speaker. He nodded. "Let's move," he said. "We don't catch that woman and kid *and* that fuckin' loose cannon, Stan's chopper isn't going to be the only thing shot down today. *Understand?* And keep your comsets tuned. Anyone sees those three call it in. I don't want to be out here when it gets dark."

As the team spread and moved into the forest Sprague glanced back at the lone figure of Stan, the pilot. The guy was sitting on a tree stump, staring at the still-smoking helicopter.

Lucky mother, Sprague thought. *All he has to worry about is that damn aluminum can. Me, I got Vigo Stone all over my ass. Christ, Stan, who has the better deal?*

16

Bolan didn't question Rachel's chosen way. She seemed to know exactly where she was going. Her moves were decisive. There was no hesitation in them. She had set a steady pace that was not going to exhaust them.

They were moving higher all the time, making a wide curve through dense forest, and Bolan worked out that she was taking them in the very direction she had outlined earlier.

Bolan heard a distant shout from their back trail—the Kendal crew was still behind them. Still coming on.

Tommy stayed close behind his mother, never once flagging. Bolan was impressed by the boy's stamina.

They reached the top of a rise, Rachel turning to pull Tommy the last couple of feet. Bolan saw the shock register on her face as she looked beyond his shoulder.

"Cooper," she yelled in warning.

Bolan brought the MP-5 on line, turning himself to check behind. He saw a teamed pair of the ground crew breaking out of the foliage, weapons up and ready to fire.

"Keep going," he called and saw Rachel and the boy vanish over the lip of the rise. He spun around to face the oncoming shooters, the MP-5 rising and snapping off a burst that caught the closest shooter in the chest. The guy spun away, a trail of misty red erupting from his back as 9 mm slugs blew out between his shoulders. The shooter's partner came at Bolan in a fevered rush, moving fast as he pounded across the open slope. He had discarded his own SMG and was dragging a SIG Sauer from his side holster. Bolan didn't give him time to use it. He leveled the H&K and hit the guy head-on with a long burst. The man seemed to go down in a ponderous fall, his jaw hitting the ground first, bone shattering as it slammed against the hard earth. The rest of his body struck the ground, slithering forward, arms flailing in a loose manner.

Bolan followed where Rachel and Tommy had dropped out of sight beyond the lip, seeing them ahead of him, still moving. They were doing exactly what he had told them to—keep running and not look back.

He used the brief clear window to reload his SMG, pushing the empty mag into a holder on his combat harness, then extracting a fresh one. As he worked it into place and cocked the weapon Bolan was doing a quick calculation. He had a full mag in the weapon and two in reserve. Three for the Beretta, plus what remained in the one in place. Bolan still didn't know the full number of men chasing them, even after just reducing the figure by two. He was up against an adversary—Senator Kendal—who had vast resources at his disposal. Kendal could bring in additional guns at will. Money was no object and the kind of men he hired would do anything if the price was accommodating.

Given that Ray Logan's evidence had the potential to tear down everything Kendal had built, one could safely assume that the man would go to extreme lengths to protect himself and the people involved in his schemes.

And if it meant eliminating Logan, his wife and his son, then that was how it would have to be.

Senator Tyrone Kendal, Bolan had learned in the short time he had been involved, was a man who never let anything, or anyone, stand in his way.

Marty Keegan had died violently.

Logan himself, severely wounded, was under threat.

And so were Rachel and Tommy Logan—caught up in the

brutal need of one man to hide his secrets and protect the corruption and deceit that accompanied his lifestyle.

Bolan was right in the middle of it all. He had put himself in the firing line because he had allied himself to Logan. Placing himself in danger didn't bother Bolan. It was an almost daily occurrence for the Executioner. It was how he operated: taking on other people's struggles when they were unable to do so themselves. He saw injustice and he reacted. If that meant he attracted opposition, he accepted that. It was simply a matter of drawing a line in the sand and standing firm. Giving in to evil only encouraged it. Cutting it down was Bolan's answer. Removing it once and for all was the practical approach.

Beyond the top of the slope the forest thinned out for a distance, exposing an uneven stretch of grassy earth. Twenty yards ahead the forest grew thick and green again, with dense undergrowth. Bolan headed for it, having spotted where Rachel and Tommy had breached the outer growth, snapping twigs and leafy tendrils. Rachel's forestry training would normally have allowed her to pass that way without disturbing too much foliage. This time she was running for her life, and the life of her son, so woodcraft stayed low on her list of priorities.

Bolan moved in among the trees, noticing the sudden silence. He should have heard Rachel and Tommy's movement ahead of him. The quiet warned him. Something was wrong.

He came to a stop, then eased off to the side, away from the trail Rachel had been moving along. Bolan began a wide circling move that would eventually bring him on a parallel track, some twenty feet to the right.

He moved without sound, and long-instilled skills came into play, skills that had served Bolan well in scenarios like this on many occasions. He would have required the fingers of both hands to list the global spots where he had acquired this particular trait.

No more than four minutes had passed when Bolan spotted the tight group.

Rachel and Tommy, on their knees, hands clasped behind their heads. He felt a moment of anger at the way they were being treated—like captives. The anger subsided with the same heartbeat. The men who had them under their guns looked on the woman and boy as just that.

Captives.

Prisoners.

Hostages to whatever sick scheme they had in mind. He knew what that was, too. Rachel and Tommy were bait to draw him in. They might have captured their prize, but they wanted Bolan out of their hair, as well. He had already raised the body count, so they would not rest easy until he was eliminated.

The pair of Kendal's men had moved fast, obviously circling around in a sweep that took them ahead of their quarry before allowing them to close in.

Down low Bolan edged closer and heard one of the men on his comset. Bolan couldn't make out any of the words, but he guessed the guy was likely calling in that they had captured Rachel and Tommy. And probably asking for additional backup and a way out of the forest since their chopper was down.

How close was backup?

Minutes away?

Longer?

Bolan realized he had no choice. He had to make his move this second. While there were only the two of them.

He observed the setup. One guy was speaking into his comset. He had shoulder-hung his SMG. As long as he was speaking, his attention would be drawn away from the prisoners, leaving his partner to watch over them. The second guy had his SMG loosely trained on the back of Rachel's head. Thinking it through, Bolan surmised that even if something went down, Rachel and Tommy would not be summarily executed. The main purpose of them being caught was to keep them alive. Bolan didn't eliminate the risk of injury to the pair. In a confrontational situation things could change with dramatic swiftness. It was hard to figure out how any individual might react to a sudden change in the situation. People reacted differently. For whatever reason, the finger on a trigger might still be pulled without thought.

Bolan took it all in, his mind snapping through the permutations, and he chose his way instinctively. Combat decisions more often than not were made quickly.

See.

Think.

Act.

Do it before the moment was snatched away.

Before the other guy had time to make *his* choice.

The window was always that thin, and when a life hung in the balance choices were thin enough to be transparent.

Bolan's finger eased the SMG's selector to single shot. He didn't want a burst of fire that might send a slug off trajectory. He needed accuracy. He was well inside the SMG's range. Close enough for dependable velocity.

Once his choice was made Bolan went ahead.

He pushed to his feet so he was in the clear. No low branches, or undergrowth to snag his clothing.

He shouldered the SMG and took aim.

The distant target caught the movement. His gaze drew from Rachel and settled on Bolan.

Bolan's finger stroked the trigger. He felt the recoil as the weapon nudged his shoulder.

The 9 mm slug struck just above the left eye and impacted against the guy's skull. It deformed on impact, twisting violently as it passed through the brain and took out a sizable chunk of the back of the guy's head. The man arched back, dropping hard.

The casing was still falling as Bolan altered his aim, tracking in on the second guy. The SMG cracked twice. Both slugs coring in through the back of the man's head and pitching him facedown on the forest floor, his body jerking violently for a few seconds. His forward fall concealed the ragged end result of the 9 mm slugs bursting out through his face.

Bolan was on the move by this time, urging Rachel and the boy away from the scene. He didn't allow them time to dwell on what had happened. And he knew that numbers were falling fast, their advantage lessening with the passing seconds.

They paralleled the edge of a steep drop, water glinting at the bottom. To their other side the ground rose in a tree-dotted slope. Light glanced through the dense mass of vegetation, making a crisscross pattern of dark and light.

Bolan didn't spot the figure barreling down the slope, on a trajectory that would bring him directly into their path. When the soldier did see the man it was a millisecond before the hurtling figure slammed into him, driving the breath from Bolan's body. Bolan remembered the drop-off. If his adversary had spotted it he hadn't allowed for it being so close. The pair of them went over the edge in a wild tumble, each man trying to gain the upper hand while attempting to maintain control of their fall.

They failed on both counts.

The loose surface off the drop cushioned Bolan as he landed. He felt his momentum increase as he slid farther down the slope. He let his body go slack, loosening his muscles so the impact was not too severe. He tried a couple of times to delay his downward fall by grabbing at anything he could. Nothing helped. Out of the corner of his eye he spotted the guy who had slammed into him. It was a blurred view of the man, but he looked to be as helpless as Bolan, bouncing and twisting as he slithered down the drop. Bolan twisted himself round and saw the bottom of the slope coming up fast. He spat out dirt that had gotten into his mouth. Bolan attempted to bring his body under control before he struck bottom…it came faster than he had anticipated. Bolan slammed into the base of the slope, his entire body jarred from the impact, and he was still rolling forward, unable to stop and found himself half submerged in the water he had seen at the bottom of the drop. The water was waist-deep and chill.

Bolan got his feet under him, pushing up out of the water. He sensed movement close by, swiveling at the waist in time to see his adversary lunging at him, big hands splayed wide apart. If the guy had been carrying, he'd lost his weapon during the fall. He slammed into Bolan, fingers clawing at the Executioner's throat. Bolan dropped his chin to his chest, denying the man a solid grip. He drove his right fist into the guy's ribs, drawing a grunt from the man. They grappled briefly, each going for a superior hold. The guy was large and solid with plenty of muscle power. He tried to slam a knee into Bolan, but the drag of the water reduced the force of his blow. Even so, Bolan felt the impact of a hard knee against his hip. Bolan planted his left hand against his opponent's broad chest and pushed him away, far enough for him to swing his bunched right fist into the guy's face. The blow landed hard, mashing lips and driving them back against the man's teeth. Blood began to dribble from the guy's mouth. He shook his head, blood spraying. He launched himself at Bolan again, the impact solid when their bodies clashed. There was no time for fancy moves. There was no telling if there were more of Kendal's people closing in and Bolan's priority was keeping Rachel and Tommy with him. Bolan drew his head back and then forward, butting the big man's nose hard. He felt it collapse and the guy roared in pain. Blood flowed copiously, streaking his lower face. The crushed nose made his opponent pause, allowing Bolan time to step back, then reach for the Tanto sheathed on his thigh. Bolan drew the blade, driving it forward. The cold steel sank to the handle in the big man's torso. He gave a trembling cry, coming to a complete standstill, staring at Bolan with shock in his eyes. He seemed about to say something, but the words never came. Bolan had already withdrawn the blade in the still of the moment. He brought it up and pulled it across the guy's throat. The cut was deep, slicing apart everything in its path. The big man clutched at the gaping wound, blood sputtering and spurting between his fingers.

Bolan stepped out of the water, putting away the Tanto. He checked his Beretta—still in its holster—then eased the strap-hung MP-5 into place. He turned back to the slope he'd just come down and started to climb. Behind him there was a heavy splash as the big man toppled over, his blood staining the water. The slope was soft underfoot so Bolan had little difficulty negotiating it. He caught sight of Rachel and Tommy standing at the top. The boy had his face pressed against his mother and Rachel had her pistol in her right hand. The expression on her face was a mix of anxiety and some shock.

She stared at Bolan, seeing the grazes and bruises he hadn't even begun to register. "You okay?"

Bolan brushed his fingers through his hair, shaking loose the debris. "That wouldn't have been my choice of getting down that slope," he said.

"Matt, you could have been badly injured," she said. "Or worse. Are you sure you're okay? No broken ribs? Concussion?"

"Rachel, I'm fine. How's Tommy?"

The boy glanced round and stared at Bolan. "That was some fall," he said. "Did you deal with the other guy?"

"Let's just be grateful Mr. Cooper isn't hurt, Tommy."

"I think it's time we moved on," Bolan said. He patted the boy's shoulder. "Let's go, Tommy."

"Will we get out of here before dark? Mom always told me it's not a good idea to go wandering around the forest then."

"If we keep moving we should reach the store just after the sun goes down," Rachel said.

"Sounds like a good plan to me," Bolan said.

They moved off again, Rachel leading them through the

trees with a confident stride, Tommy behind her and Bolan, ever watchful, bringing up the rear.

He didn't discount the possibility of further action. Bolan never did rely on laxity. It was when a man's guard was down that problems arose.

So Bolan walked on with caution, his attention at full stretch. And he didn't let his guard down even when they reached the store just after dark started to fall across the forest.

17

Light shone from the store windows. Smoke curled from the chimney. The place gave out an atmosphere of calm. As they moved toward the store Rachel gave a sigh of relief, drawing Tommy close.

"We did it," she said. "Matt, we made it. You got us…"

Bolan didn't reply. He put out a warning arm to hold them back.

Because something wasn't right.

He couldn't have explained it in words. It was a feeling. A sense of unease. Something telling him the situation was off-kilter.

Rachel turned to stare at him, eyes wide with a perceived sense of danger. "What is it, Matt?"

Beside her Tommy looked across at Bolan's shadowed profile and stayed silent himself.

Bolan brought the MP-5 into play, making no sudden moves as he scanned the store and the surrounding terrain. With darkness starting to fall, shadows had already deepened so his sight was restricted. If there was anyone watching them they would be hidden in the gloom. None of the other cabins showed any light. No sign of movement, and Bolan recalled Sarah telling him there were no other occupants in residence at this time.

Keeping her voice low Rachel asked, "What do we do?"

"We need to back up. Into the trees so we have cover."

"No. That is not what you should do."

The voice behind Bolan came with an unmistakably Russian accent, the words delivered slowly because the speaker still hadn't fully mastered English.

The hard muzzle of a weapon was jammed into Bolan's spine. There was no need for any translation there—the meaning was clear. Bolan took his hands from the SMG, letting it dangle from the sling. He held them out from his sides. Heroic gestures were one thing. Reckless ones were something else. As much as he wanted to take on this Russian, even the Executioner couldn't dodge a bullet at such close range.

The Russian took Bolan's weapons. One by one—MP-5, Beretta, the Tanto knife.

Out of the corner of his eye Bolan made visual contact with Tommy. The boy stared back at him, a silent message going between them. He nodded briefly.

"Inside the cabin," the Russian said, pushing the muzzle against Bolan to emphasize his command.

"We have to do as he says, Rachel," Bolan said. He took a step forward, saw Rachel do the same. Then Bolan simply said, "Tommy, *go. Hide.*"

The boy didn't hesitate. He turned about and with the agility of a ten-year-old he ran, fast, back to the trees, his slim form vanishing in the darkness. He disappeared in seconds, losing himself in the undergrowth.

"Hey," the Russian yelled. He gave a frustrated growl and Bolan felt the uncompromising slam of the weapon the man held as he drove it against his spine. The blow hurt. Bolan sucked in his breath, stumbling briefly.

"Matt," he heard Rachel cry.

"Woman, you shut your mouth. Now get inside cabin before I kill you both."

There was nothing else either of them could do. With the armed man at their backs Bolan and Rachel were marched up to the store.

As they reached the door the Russian behind Bolan yelled out an order, and Bolan realized he was giving orders to others on the far side of the cabin. The Executioner's Russian allowed him a sketchy translation. It increased the odds against Bolan if these others came into the store.

As he and Rachel were forced inside, the scene that unfolded was far from promising. Arthur and Sarah Kenner were seated by the counter. They looked tired and scared. There were three more Russians nearby, SMGs hanging from their shoulders. The guy Bolan had overpowered and tied up, had apparently been freed and was also there. One of the Russian heavies came forward and took the confiscated weapons he was handed. He dropped them on the store counter.

Kendal's man, a pleased smirk on his face, walked across to Bolan and Rachel. The smirk vanished when he realized Rachel was on her own.

"Where's the brat?" he asked.

The Russian behind Bolan said, "He ran off. Back into the forest. I could not stop him."

"What the hell. He's just a fuckin' kid." He laughed at something. "Hey, maybe the bears will get him. Park Rangers will find his bones."

The Russian gave a hoarse chuckle. "*Da*. That would be good." He stepped around Bolan and stood beside Kendal's man. "This the one who tie you up, Lohman?"

Lohman fingered his marked face, recalling what Bolan had done. "I owe you," he said to Bolan.

"My one mistake," Bolan said. "I didn't hit you hard enough."

Lohman gave an angry yell and launched himself forward, swinging wildly with a .357 mm SIG Sauer pistol clutched in his hand. His attack was fuelled by rage, losing him any form of control, and Bolan neatly sidestepped, reaching up to grab Lohman's right arm. He used his grip to drag Lohman closer, sweeping up his own right arm in a forearm smash that contacted Lohman's cheek. The blow reopened the gash in Lohman's cheek, blood spurting down his face. Bolan hauled the dazed man in close, neatly stepping behind him, snatching the SIG from Lohman's loose grip.

The Russian who had brought Bolan and Rachel into the cabin was lifting the SMG in his hands when Bolan shot him, the SIG making a loud sound within the confines of the store. The slug hammered into the Russian's chest, making him step back, his face registering surprise, then pain. Bolan triggered three more shots into the guy, dropping him where he stood.

Rachel had thrown herself clear, letting her body drop to the floor, giving Bolan a clear field of fire.

He felt Lohman shudder as one of the Russians opened fire from across the store. His shots hit Lohman and the man started to sag in Bolan's grip. As Lohman dropped, Bolan swung the SIG low, angling the muzzle beneath Lohman's arm, triggering as fast as he was able. The Russian shooter grunted under the impact of the .357 mm slugs. He staggered backward, bloody shreds blowing out between his shoulders.

A second Russian hauled his SMG up from hip level, stepping forward to track Bolan's prone body.

Sarah Kenner thrust out a booted foot that tripped the shooter. He almost went down on his knees but recovered his balance. With a harsh curse on his lips he swung around and triggered the SMG, laying down a burst of auto fire that blew the helpless woman off her chair. The Russian held his finger against the trigger, his anger making him forget Bolan as he fired into Arthur Kenner.

Bolan was already pushing up off the floor, his right hand aiming the SIG at the Russian. He placed two .357 slugs into the back of the man's broad skull, the powerful bullets taking the Russian's head apart in a burst of bloody bone and brain matter.

Bolan felt the slide of the SIG lock back and realized the weapon had not been holding a full magazine. He tossed the gun aside, starting to rise to his feet as the third Russian, his SMG out of reach on the counter, snatched a wooden ax-handle out of a barrel at his side and headed for Bolan at a full run, ready to strike. On one knee Bolan let him come, then reached out to grab the guy's flapping coat the moment the Russian made a wild swing with the wooden club. Bolan dragged the Russian with him, falling to the floor and bringing up his right foot. He planted the sole of his boot in the man's stomach, thrusting up and back. He went hurtling over Bolan, letting go a startled scream as he was projected through the air, hitting one of the store's windows full on. Glass shattered, wood splintered and the Russian flew out of sight. Bolan rolled to his right, gaining his feet and snatched up one of the dropped SMGs. He handed it to Rachel as she stood.

"Get over by the far wall," he said.

Bolan spotted the Kenners' Winchester on the counter and grabbed it as he heard bootsteps on the porch outside the door. The voices calling out were Russian.

The door was kicked in, dark shapes filling the opening. Bolan saw a grim-faced Russian storming in his direction. The guy wielded an SMG and he jerked on the trigger as Bolan ducked low. The stream of slugs chewed raw slivers of wood from the door frame. Staying low, Bolan triggered a 12-gauge shell into the guy. At close range the effect was devastating, ripping open the Russian's torso and taking out a section of his ribs. The power of the shot threw him off the porch and he slammed to the ground, blood and insides streaming in his wake. A second guy, yelling in a wild, guttural voice, was too late to stop his forward movement. He tried to jerk away from the open door but was too slow for the Executioner's adrenaline-powered reaction. The Winchester tracked a few inches to the left, Bolan tripping the trigger even as he caught a glimpse of the shooter's SMG. The full charge of the 12-gauge blast took him in the left shoulder, tearing at muscle, bone and flesh. The guy's arm was ripped free, hand still clutching at his SMG, as blood began to fountain from the severed shoulder. Bolan, harboring no kind of forgiveness, hit the guy with a second shot, blowing him off the porch with half his skull missing.

Raised voices caught Bolan's attention. They came from his left. Bolan knew it would not be long before those voices became solid shapes as the Russians came at him.

He ducked out of the door, moving right along the porch, taking a leap over the end rail. He landed hard, let himself tuck and roll, keeping the shotgun tight to his chest. As he uncurled, he saw the moving Russians heading in his direction, then running up onto the porch.

Rising to his feet, Bolan faced his attackers and let rip with the auto shotgun, riddling the porch and the men with 12-gauge death. He saw his shots hit home, blood and flesh misting the air as the Russians tumbled awkwardly. Their screams and shouts were lost in the boom of the lethal shots. Behind the falling Russians, Bolan saw two figures draw back, away from the porch, and move back in the direction they had come from.

As one of the dead Russians flopped loosely over the edge of the porch his SMG slipped from slack fingers. Bolan dropped the shotgun and snatched up the weapon, checking the magazine as he skirted the edge of the porch in pursuit of the survivors. He had to keep up the pressure. Maintain his advantage, thin as it was.

Bolan sprinted across the front of the cabin. Saw one of the Russians as he picked up the sound of pursuit, turning to face Bolan. Bolan triggered the SMG, stitching the guy hard across belly and chest. The Russian staggered under the impact, still fighting on. Bolan had to hit him again, slugs coring in and tearing at his throat and head. The guy went down hard.

IN THE DARKNESS, farther back from where Bolan had left his own vehicle, the surviving Russian had reached a pair of high-spec 4x4s. He caught sight of the American closing in, searching for him. He moved quickly, dipping into deep shadow, using the bulk of the two vehicles to conceal him. He knew what he was doing, falling back on evasive maneuvers drilled into him during a long stint in the Russian military. He watched the man he knew as Cooper sliding from shadow to shadow, acknowledging the enemy's skill. He could understand how Cooper had defeated every one of Kendal's and

Koretski's men. He was a warrior. An elusive fighter. A man to be respected and feared. To be treated with caution.

The Russian, named Borodin, eased his way around until he was behind the American. It took all his skill and nerve. And it took time, something Borodin had only a little of to spare. He was thinking about the Logan woman. The target of the foray into the forest. He had seen her taken inside the store, but she had not come out. If she was still in there, waiting for Cooper, there was a chance of capturing her alive. That was his sole reason for being here. To take the woman and deliver her to his employer—Maxim Koretski.

Koretski would get the woman to talk. To tell where the evidence the cop had gathered was. Everything centered around that evidence. Right now nothing else mattered.

Only the woman.

The evidence.

Borodin saw a figure emerge from inky blackness.

Cooper.

A smile edged his lips. The man was closer than he had realized, and Borodin was still behind him. Two, three steps, and he would be close enough to touch the big American—close enough that a quick burst from his SMG would end the affair. Borodin held off from the trigger. Shots might only startle the woman into reacting. Perhaps cause her to run before he could reach her. Borodin's mind worked quickly. His only weapon was the SMG. He had no knife, no handgun. So he would have to use what he held in his hands.

The Russian rose to his full height, taking a long step that brought him closer to the tall American. Borodin swung the SMG in a powerful arc, smashing it against the rear of Cooper's skull. He heard the man grunt from the solid impact, and just to be sure, he struck again, even harder, and Cooper fell to his knees, then went facedown on the forest floor.

Borodin stood over the motionless figure for a moment. He saw blood glistening beneath the thick black hair. He would have liked to have gotten to know the big American. To have spoken to him. He imagined Cooper would have been an interesting conversationalist.

The Russian stepped away, turning in the direction of the store, and went to find the woman.

18

It took Bolan no time at all to find Tommy Logan. The boy had done exactly what he had been told—run and hide. His understanding was that Bolan would come and find him when the danger was gone. Which is what he did. The boy was concealed deep in a tangled thicket and even Bolan didn't see him until his call brought Tommy to his side.

"You have blood running down your face," Tommy stated, pointing at where it had seeped from his hairline.

"I think I upset someone."

Tommy shook his head. "You seem to do that a lot, Mr. Cooper."

Bolan smiled, despite the savage headache left behind after the Russian had laid him out. He needed to tend to the wound. His first response when he woke up had been to go to the store and look for Rachel, but he'd suspected she would already be gone. When he had stepped inside the store his suspicions were confirmed, and Bolan was confronted by the dead. He ignored the Russians and the man called Lohman. His only concern was for Sarah Kenner and her husband. He stood over their bloody bodies, a feeling of outrage growing at their senseless deaths. Two good people who had, by a simple chance of fate, been dragged into the ugly world of Tyrone Kendal and Maxim Koretski. Violent death had been visited upon two innocents, and Bolan was once again left to mourn their passing.

Bolan located a stack of blankets on one of the shelves and

gently covered their bodies. He stood, head bowed, and made them a promise.

"They won't go unpunished. I promise you that."

He retrieved his weapons, and that was when a sound behind Bolan made him turn, Beretta in his fist. One of the Russians had made the sound, almost a whisper that might have gone unnoticed if there had been any other noise inside the store. Bolan went to stand over the man. He was bloody and weak from the .357 slugs Bolan had put into him.

"Help me," he said in a grating whisper.

"You first," Bolan said, crouching by the man. "Where were they taking the woman?"

The Russian stared at Bolan as if he didn't understand. He was close to death and most likely didn't care about Rachel Logan.

"You know what I'm asking," Bolan said. "You get nothing until I have an answer."

"To Koretski's base. You call it the Cascades."

The Cascade Mountains. Up country. Plenty of isolated areas.

"Where in the Cascades?"

Bolan received no answer. He bent over the Russian. The man had expired.

On his feet Bolan stood for a moment, swaying as a dizzy spell swept over him. He let the moment pass, then turned and went back outside to get Tommy.

He took the boy into the store by the rear door and got him seated in front of the hearth by the burning log fire. He then closed the door that led through into the store.

The living area incorporated a neat kitchen, which Bolan made use of by putting water on the stove to heat.

"Mr. Cooper, where's my mom?"

It was the question he had been anticipating. Bolan had dampened a towel and had it pressed to the gash in his head. "Those men took her away, Tommy. They did bad things here and took her away before I could stop them."

"You going to help get her back? Like you did before?"

"I'm going to get her back, Tommy."

"Then that's okay."

Bolan wished reality was as cut and dry.

He had lost his sat phone somewhere along the way during the hectic and bloody events, so he picked up the Kenners' landline phone and tapped in a long number sequence. He hadn't used the number for a long time but it still worked and eventually he was connected to Stony Man Farm.

He spoke to Barbara Price, telling her what he needed. "This has to be fast, Barb. I need to be on the road as soon as possible, but I can't leave a ten-year-old boy here on his own. Work through Hal. Get local Feds up here—the works if you need to. But I need Hal to know I can't be held while they ask their questions. Pull Leo in if you have to. Justice can work the strings."

"Hey, slow down, Striker. You sound like you're wired. Are you okay?"

"I took a whack on the head is all. I'm brewing up some strong coffee. I'll be fine once I down a couple of pints."

"How long do you think you can go on like this? And just what *is* going on out there?"

"I don't have time to explain everything. I want you to talk to Bear. He'll give you exact directions that you can pass on to the Feds to get here."

Price disregarded all protocol. "Mack, I'm worried about you. Please take care."

"Don't I always?" The moment he said the words, Bolan tried to imagine what Price would say if she learned about everything he'd been through recently. "Have a talk with Bear. He has a little background on this."

"Great," Price said. "Gee, I'm only the mission controller so what do I know?"

"This blew up fast," Bolan said. "Didn't leave me much time to brief everyone." He gave Price Ray Logan's location at Doc Madsen's and what he had arranged. "If you really want to know the skinny, have a talk with Ray. He'll tell you everything. But keep it under the radar. Inside The Farm."

"Got it, Striker. Anything else you need from the Feds?"

"I lost my sat phone. It went missing during…along the way."

"Sit tight. I'll get the local Seattle field office to take a call from Hal and Leo." There was a pause, then, "Take care, Striker."

The call ended and Bolan put down the phone.

"Mr. Cooper. Is Barb your girlfriend?"

A candid question that could only have come from a ten-year-old.

"Sometimes," he answered.

Bolan made a pot of coffee. He sat down, feeling like the top of his head was about to explode. He emptied his mug and went for a refill. When he passed the couch he saw that Tommy was asleep. He looked down at the boy. That was the way to do it, he decided. Put all your problems on hold and sleep. He downed a second mug of coffee.

A thought was turning over in his mind. A possible solution to a problem he had even forgotten to take up with Stony Man Farm.

Bolan draped a blanket over Tommy, then made his way out through the store and walked to where the Russian SUVs had been parked. Only one remained. A big black Chevy Suburban. The other would have been taken by the man who had snatched Rachel.

He slipped into the driver's seat and powered the vehicle up. As the dashboard lights came on Bolan spotted what he was looking for—the built-in navigation system. He checked out the display. It showed the SUV's present position. Bolan tapped the touch screen and from the list of destinations he chose the one marked Home. He watched the display change as the satellites began to chart the designated return route. It showed the main highway with the previous route in reverse, and in a few moments Bolan had his way to Maxim Koretski's base on screen.

Two hours on and Bolan was burning rubber north as he took up the route that would deliver him to Maxim Koretski's

home base. While he had waited for the cavalry to arrive he
had transferred his ordnance and luggage from his own rental
to the Chevy SUV. The vehicle was the top-of-the-range
model, fitted with everything any self-respecting Russian
Mafiya member could want. Koretski obviously didn't hold
back when it came to outfitting his work crews.

After his call to Stony Man Farm, Bolan had retired to the
bathroom and cleaned up the gash on his head. It wasn't easy
but any more medical assistance would have to wait. At least
the wound had stopped bleeding and the pounding headache
had slowed to a bearable level. He caught sight of himself in
the mirror as he toweled his face dry after a wash. He was
showing a number of bruises and scrapes and he needed a
shave.

"This line of work isn't doing much for your good looks,"
he said to himself, offering his battered image a wry grin.

In the store Bolan took some bottled water from the chill
cabinet and added a handful of nutrient bars. He went out and
placed them in the SUV, checked his watch and went back
to move Tommy. He wrapped the sleeping boy in his blanket
and carried him out to the SUV, laying him across the rear
seat. He fired up the Chevy's engine and drove it to the fuel
pumps near the store. Bolan filled the tank to the top. Back
behind the wheel he swung the SUV round and headed back
down the dark trail until he reached the main highway where
he parked and waited.

THE AGENT IN THE LEAD CAR of a convoy of five, all showing
flashing lights, stepped out to meet the man he was to know
as Matt Cooper. He was a fair-haired man around Bolan's
height, wearing an FBI jacket over his suit. He took a long
look at Bolan's dark attire and weapons but said nothing after
introducing himself as Harry Jessup.

"Look after the boy," Bolan said. "He's had a rough time."

A female agent took Tommy to the FBI car. "He'll be
fine," she said.

Jessup handed Bolan a sat phone. "I was asked to give you this, Cooper." He hesitated. "And told not to ask questions."

"That make you feel out of the loop?" Bolan asked lightly.

Jessup smiled. "Kind of."

"When you reach the store up along that trail you're going to have plenty to pull you back in again."

Bolan raised his hand as he turned and headed back to his parked SUV. Moments later he had pulled onto the highway, the Chevy's powerful headlights carving his route through the darkness.

Bolan put in a call to Stony Man Farm and the cyber unit. Kurtzman answered his call.

"Thanks for getting me chewed out by the fair Barbara. She can let off steam once she works it up. So what can I tell you this time, Striker?"

"That you have an update on Maxim Koretski. About his home base up in the Cascades."

"House used to belong to some megarich businessman back in the 1930s. Shipping magnate. Built the place to impress his second wife. It didn't work. The house was too isolated so she upped and went back to high society. Since then the place has had a number of owners until Koretski's buyout a few years ago. Big mansion. Sits in its own grounds so you can't just walk up to the front door and ask to be let in."

"Got it."

"So what's going on, Striker?"

"A cover-up? Too much happening that's a little too convenient? Makes me wonder, Bear. Or do I just have a suspicious mind?"

"Yes, you do. And it usually turns out to have the truth in there somewhere."

19

Jakob Binder had started the whole thing off. He was into Maxim Koretski for a fortune. Binder had a chronic gambling obsession. He was the kind of man who would bet on the fall of a leaf dropping from a tree. The unfortunate thing was that he lost more than he won. A couple of times he had made good, but his weakness was his inability to take his winnings and quit while he was ahead. He had to go for the next jackpot, and without fail he would gamble his winnings away.

Binder's other weaknesses were drink and a pretty face—a lethal combination when coupled with his gambling. One of Koretski's girls, a delightful, elfin-faced young beauty named Katrina, had hooked him early. She'd flattered him, seduced him and encouraged his vices. When Binder got in too deep, she introduced him to Koretski, who made sympathetic noises, promised he would help, and opened a credit line for the man. Binder was allowed to make a few wins, but over a two-month period his losses mounted until he owed Koretski enough money to have bought a midsize condo.

That was when the trap snapped shut.

Binder was so much in debt, his markers in Koretski's possession, that his life belonged to the Russian. His situation was finally brought into the open the day Katrina took him for a meeting with Koretski at his office on the top floor of the Russian's business HQ overlooking the Seattle waters.

"What does Maxim want?"

Katrina, standing beside him in the elevator, smiled. "He

has a little surprise for you," she purred. Her soft voice, with its hint of an accent, matched her looks. "You must wait and see."

Binder couldn't see her face at that moment. If he had, he might have been shocked at the cold, unfeeling look in her eyes. She walked out of the elevator ahead of him, directly into Koretski's sprawling office. A wide, panoramic window looked out across the city and the bay. The office was expensively furnished, with a reception area to one side.

Koretski lounged in a large, soft leather executive chair, a welcoming smile on his face. There were four other men in the room, watching Binder.

One of them seemed vaguely familiar. Binder stared at him for a few moments, then realized he was looking at Senator Tyrone Kendal. The sight of the senator made Binder uneasy. He knew of the man's reputation. Kendal was an uncompromisingly hard man who worked tirelessly for his constituents, but harder for his own aggrandizement. So what was he doing in the company of someone like Koretski?

Binder had a feeling he was about to find out, and wouldn't like the answer.

"Please sit down, Jakob," Koretski said. After Binder took one of the comfortable matching seats in front of Koretski's massive desk, the Russian leaned forward, face solemn. "I have a proposition for you, Jakob, and I want you to consider before you make any answer. We have a mutual problem. A simple one. You have accumulated an extremely large gambling debt, and you owe that debt to me. I have your markers, which you willingly signed and I must say that a degree of recklessness on your part has allowed that debt to spiral out of control. My accountant here, Oleg," he said, indicating a slim, pale-faced young man holding a large ledger, "has estimated that your current salary would not make much of a dent in what you owe if you were able to remain in employment for the next fifty years. That is a conservative estimate, based on the fact you are already in your fortieth year. Did I not mention the interest you will also need to pay on the loan?

So, Jakob, I am sure you see the problem. How do I recoup my investment? Which brings us to my proposition."

Silence enveloped the room, broken only when Katrina moved and crossed to the generous wet bar close by. She took a bottle and poured a generous amount of bourbon into a thick tumbler and offered it to Binder, who took it a little too eagerly, gulping noisily as he swallowed half the amount.

"He drinks like a fish," Katrina said, making no attempt to hide the contempt in her suddenly hard voice. "And he spills a lot when he has had too much. Maxim, I should be angry at you for making me play up to this loser over the last few months."

Binder turned to stare at her. At the once-pretty face, hardened into a cold mask. Realization hit him like a punch to the stomach.

"But you said…"

She laughed. "I said I loved you," she mocked, her voice taking on a harsh Russian tone. "He begged me to say it every time we were in bed. God, it makes me shudder when I think about it."

"All in a day's work," Koretski said. "And you did it so well, my dear." Koretski chuckled. "We have it all on disc so I appreciate how much effort you put into it."

"*You* didn't have him drooling and pawing over you," Katrina said.

Koretski smiled across at the white-faced Binder. "So, Jakob, where do we go from here?"

Binder drained his glass. He barely noticed when Katrina took the empty tumbler, refilled it and returned it to him.

"I think he has lost the power of speech," she said.

"Well, he'd better get it back damn fast," Senator Kendal said, moving to stand beside Koretski's desk. "Let's cut the crap, Maxim. I understand this little shit has most of his brains in his pants, but there must be some left in his head so he can figure out what's coming next."

"Not exactly the way I would have phrased it," Koretski said, "but I understand what you are getting at. Jakob, it is quite simple. I own you now. Unless you prefer the quick way out, which I doubt, there may be something we can do to ease your problem."

Binder focused on the Russian. He took another drink. "What?"

"It has to do with your work with the oil commission."

Binder frowned. "I don't understand."

"You work for the Department of the Interior. You have influence," Koretski said. "You have access to confidential files. You can effect changes."

Kendal reached out and handed Binder a computer printout. The man ran his gaze over the text, surprised at what he saw.

"How did you get hold of this? It's supposed to be highly classified. There are no more than three people who know about it."

"You're one," Kendal said. "Berkowski and Reynolds are the others. I'll let you try and figure out the one who brought this to me. Suffice it to say it was offered in the hope the offender might reduce *his* liability to us," Kendal said.

"We haven't decided yet how to reward him for this information. His influence is far lower on the scale than yours. Which is why we turned to you," Koretski said.

"How many people are there on your payroll?" Binder asked.

"That's something you'll never get to know."

Binder looked at Koretski. The Russian shrugged. "He won't even tell me. Just a word of caution, Jakob. You have family. Two sisters. Both married. They have children. Husbands. Your mother lives in Vermont. I mention this simply as a cautionary matter. If you think of revealing our conversation here today, or any of the people present, then believe it when I say I would be extremely disappointed and forced to make reprisals. Do I make myself understood?"

Binder nodded. "Yes. I understand."

"And do not fool yourself into believing if you decided it was all too much and did away with yourself I would spare your family—don't. Try to cheat me, and I will still make them pay."

Binder's expression was pitiful. A trapped man, caught in the spotlight. Helpless.

"I'm glad we have that cleared up. Now we can work out how you can help the senator and myself."

"What is it you want?" Binder asked. He expected the worst, and that was exactly what he got.

The next few weeks were a nightmare as Binder manipulated reports and figures. He altered geological surveys and had physical samples sent to his department substituted with false ones. He worked harder discounting the claims and suggestions than he had ever worked before. It was difficult but not impossible. Federal cutbacks meant a smaller staff. Binder had always made himself indispensable, so his apparent attention to detail was not suspected as being anything but normal.

When the report came in that a light plane carrying a survey team had crashed with total loss of life in Alaska, he failed to realize the implications at first. It was only later that the truth clicked in and he realized it had been no accident. The three men and one woman on the flight had been involved in the original survey. It had been their findings that had generated first interest in the new field. They had been out in the field since submitting the reports, so none of them were aware of Binder's manipulation.

His shock forced him to contact Koretski. The Russian had asked what he wanted.

"I think you know," Binder said. "The plane crash."

Koretski had been silent for a moment. "Say no more. A car will come for you shortly. Speak to no one."

Binder was picked up at a prearranged spot and driven to Koretski's building. When he stepped from the elevator into Koretski's office the first person he saw was Katrina. Her smile was cool, her manner disdainful.

"Do you miss me, Jakob?"

"Katrina, behave yourself," Koretski said. "Jakob is upset about something. Come and sit down, Jakob."

Binder took the same seat he had used all those weeks earlier. He was nervous. His emotions were all over the place. The revelation he had come to accept as true manifested itself in severe trembling in his hands. Even Koretski noticed. He poured a tumbler full of bourbon and brought it to Binder.

"Try not to spill it on the carpet, Jakob," he said. "It cost a great deal of money." He returned to sit at his desk. "Now what has got you all agitated?"

"Did you arrange for that plane to crash? To kill those people?"

Koretski stroked his chin, as if he was considering Binder's question. "Yes, I did."

"My God. You deliberately murdered them?"

Koretski held out his hands. "Didn't I just say so? You heard me, Katrina?"

"Clearly."

"But..."

"But nothing, Jakob. The survey team could have challenged *your* misrepresentation of the facts. *Your* switching of core samples. The altering of figures. All down to you. While they were still out in the field the risk was minimal, but they were coming back, and the moment they walked into the department and saw what had happened to their reports... What the hell, Jakob? How would you talk your way out of that?"

"They were good people. They had done nothing to deserve what you did to them."

"Part of the reason I decided not to mention them before. I needed you concentrating on the matter at hand, not pining over the fate of some out-of-town coworkers. Stay focused, Jakob, and think about what happened to your team. Accidents happen all the time." Koretski smiled. "Family, Jakob. I would hate to have to start picking who should be first."

Binder stared down at the tumbler in his hands. He managed to raise it to his lips, downing the liquid in a single swallow.

"Listen to me, Jakob. Senator Kendal has some details he requires your approval on. He's negotiating the purchase of some deep-water equipment that needs a degree of official approval. His own consortium is working on, shall we say, something a little tricky, at the moment. Kendal has to stay clear of any negotiations concerning his company, since he isn't supposed to be involved due to his senatorial role. So a newly created division, not even part of his enterprises, will deal with it. Somewhere along the line they will be seeking operating licenses, which is where you will come in. You do understand, Jakob? They will be granted anything they need."

Binder understood. The new company—in essence Kendal and Koretski—would be in a position to establish the field. To take control of the exploration, development and eventual potential yield. He knew the facts and figures. The yield would be impressive. The amount of crude would translate into billions of dollars and it would be channeled into the hands of the partners. On a daily basis the whole enterprise would be managed and operated by front men, who would probably not even know who they were actually working for. The multiple layers of management, deceit and crooked operating procedures would be designed to keep Kendal and Koretski protected. The payoffs would keep everyone happy and would total out to an insignificant figure when stood against what Kendal and Koretski would be banking. Moved around the financial world, the money would be hidden from inquisitive eyes until it became invisible and the manipulations of the partners would be lost.

Binder understood he was just one of a number of individuals being used, and as long as Kendal and his Russian partner had his family under the hammer, there was nothing he could do. At the back of his mind lurked the fact that he was as vulnerable as his dead team. If—*when*—he outlived his usefulness, there would no longer be any reason why he should stay alive. Binder had no illusions about that. His life was in the hands of the men coercing him. The lives of his extended family were in *his* hands. It was a nightmare without end. One he couldn't wake up from.

20

Bolan parked the Chevy off road, hiding it in thick bushes. Instinct told him that Maxim Koretski would have watchers both inside and outside his base. The Russian was a survivor, a man who walked in a violent world, and that kind of existence brought its own paranoia. Koretski would see trouble waiting at every turn and he would make sure he was well-protected. Like most of his kind he gave out signals of confidence. A bravura to show that he was never intimidated. Never bested. Yet he would have his bodyguards around at all times.

Clad in a blacksuit and carrying his ordnance, Bolan went EVA about a half mile short of his destination. Using the night shadows he made his silent, unseen approach along the perimeter wall that flanked the road. The darkness befriended him, offering cover, merging his black garb with its own cloak. Bolan was able to come within sight of the gated entrance and the pair of armed heavies unlucky enough to have drawn the short straw. They both carried AK-74s, hooked over their shoulders by leather straps. Bolan guessed they would also have holstered handguns under their top-coats. One of them smoked continuously, lighting up a fresh cigarette each time he finished one. Both men were reaching that stage in their shift when the routine was starting to drag and they were wishing they could go back inside the house and have a hot drink. Bolan spent some time studying the patrol routine. Each man started from the gate. One walked east, the other west, until they reached the end of the front wall, then made a return to the gate. A simple routine that seemed to satisfy the guards. Bolan figured they might have a similar pair watching the back wall. He didn't intend to waste time finding out. From gate to corner the slow walk took eight minutes, and then another eight back. Time enough. Bolan waited until the pair decided to walk the walk.

The guy moving east was coming his way and Bolan met him halfway into his patrol. He was crouching in the thick grass growing at the base of the wall—the guard had no warning. Bolan simply rose to his full height as the man passed. He swung his arms around the guard's neck, pulling him into a crippling headlock. Bolan's muscles strained hard as he applied pressure. The guard had no chance to call out. His air was cut off and so was the blood flow through his arteries. As the guy went facedown Bolan jammed a knee into his spine, grasped his head and hauled back until he heard the snap of vertebrae. The guard became limp.

Bolan stripped off the dead man's thick coat and shrugged into it. He pulled on the knit cap the man had been wearing, and picked up the AK-74. Before he resumed the guard's walk, Bolan rolled the body into the cover of the thick grass at the base of the wall.

Upon completion Bolan about-turned and began to retrace the man's steps, fixing the other guard in his line of sight. He hoped the guy wasn't the talkative type. No words were spoken, even when the two were no more than a few yards apart. Bolan strolled up toward the gates, head low, the collar of his coat pulled up around his ears.

And it was then that the other guard said, "Sergei? You look taller than... You are not Sergei—"

The man snatched at his dangling auto rifle, but Bolan powered forward and slammed bodily into him. They crashed to the ground, Bolan on top, his left hand pushing the other man's weapon aside, pinning it to his body, while his right fist, bunched tight, slammed into the Russian's face. Bolan hit hard, over and over, drawing blood and breaking teeth and jaw. The Russian put up a struggle. He was strong, his wiry frame bucking and twisting beneath Bolan's solid weight. Bolan could feel the man trying to break the hold on his AK-74, desperate to reach the trigger so he could fire a warning shot. His right hand was pounding at Bolan's chest in an attempt to push Bolan off him. Feeling the Russian's closeness to the AK's trigger Bolan moved his left hand, grabbed the guy's fingers and bent them back until he heard bones crack as they snapped. The Russian let out a pained cry, blood spraying from his mouth. Before he could yell again Bolan hammered his fist down against the guy's nose, feeling it cave in. He drove his fist in again and again, cartilage breaking amid a spew of bright blood that cascaded across the Russian's face. He was choking, blood flooding his throat. His struggles became weaker. With the Russian contained, Bolan reached and slid the Tanto knife from its sheath and pushed the razor blade in deep, under the ribs and into the heart. He worked it brutally, causing fatal damage to the organ. The guard shuddered violently before slipping silently into death. Easing the knife free, Bolan wiped the blade on the grass, then returned it to its sheath.

He pushed to his feet, stepping back from the guard, and checked the closed gates. They were electronically locked. He turned his attention to the stone-block wall. It was eight feet high. Bolan slung his SMG across his back, took a few steps back and launched himself up. His fingers grasped the edge of the top stone. He hung for a moment before hauling himself bodily up the wall, using the tips of his boots to gain precious holds on the uneven surface. He rolled prone on the top of the wall, checking out the lay of the grounds. Satisfied the immediate area was clear, Bolan then lowered himself down the wall. Bolan felt his feet touch the ground. He crouched in the dark shadow at the foot of the wall, eyes searching the interlocking shadows created by the lights from the house spilling across the ground. He checked for movement but saw none. Even so, he stayed where he was for some time, never one to take things at face value. A hasty move could easily turn against him. No amount of reading the enemy could allow for an unexpected appearance, a random step taken by an enemy on the spur of the moment. Bolan let time slip by.

Watching.

Waiting.

His vigilance was rewarded as a dark shape stepped out from a small side door, the man outlined in the pale glow of light from inside the house. Bolan saw enough. A bulky physique, the configuration of an SMG held loosely in the man's hands, and then the darkness returned as the door closed behind the guy. Bolan's eyes had attuned to the gloom and he was able to track the man's movements as he walked away from the house, head moving left and right as he did. The SMG was relegated to one hand, muzzle lowered, as the guard reached inside his bulky coat and drew out a pack of cigarettes. He flipped the pack to loosen one cigarette and pulled it free with his teeth. The pack was returned to his pocket and replaced with a lighter. Flame showed as the cigarette was lit. The glowing tip became a tiny beacon for Bolan to follow as the guy paced the area.

Drawing back, Bolan positioned himself so he was able to cover the sentry's path. It dawned on him that the guy was making for the gated entrance—a security check? It offered Bolan the opportunity to take the guy out while he was a distance from the house. He stayed well to the side as he followed the man to the gates, only closing in as he shouldered his weapon, using both hands to inspect the high gates, rattling them briefly to ensure they were secured. Satisfied, the guard turned about to retrace his steps.

But before he could get any farther, Bolan materialized directly in front of the man and took a hard fist to his throat. The force of the blow was followed by the collapse of his larynx and everything around it. His ability to breathe apparently ceased and the man began to choke. The cigarette dropped from his lips. He grabbed his throat, as if hope told him it might ease the problem. It didn't. He fell back against the gates, briefly held there by the solid metal. Then he dropped to his knees, already losing consciousness.

Bolan had picked up the sentry's SMG—additional fire-power was something he would never eschew. As he closed in on the house he assessed the acquired weapon; the made-in-Belgium FN P90 was a modernistic bullpup design. Chambered for 5.7 mm ammo contained in a translucent plastic top-mounted magazine, with a 50-round capacity, capable of semi or full auto fire, this weapon had a suppressor screwed to the barrel to reduce noise. Bolan checked the weapon and found it set and ready to use. He slung his own MP-5 across his back. The fifty extra rounds the P90 would provide was not to be dismissed. As he had no idea how much opposition might be inside the house the additional ordnance was welcome.

Bolan stood against the wall next to the door the sentry had exited. He was going inside to rescue Rachel Logan. Anyone who stood in his way would pay the ultimate price. His initial attempt at bringing the woman and her son to safety had failed. He wasn't about to let that happen a second time. Bolan had made a promise to Ray Logan and he refused to accept defeat. The cop had put his life on the line in order to bring Kendal and his associates to justice. His family had been drawn into danger through his actions, and Bolan's promise to see his wife and child safely delivered back to Logan would not be allowed to fall by the wayside.

Bolan checked the door handle. It moved easily and the door swung open at his touch. He pushed it fully open, standing to one side. The lit passage ran for no more than ten feet before it terminated in a rising flight of stone steps. Bolan eased inside, closed the door, spotted a slide bolt and secured it, preventing anyone from moving in behind him. The steps led to a second door, partially open. Bolan edged it wider and checked out the hallway beyond. There was a door on either side, and the passage widened into a generous entrance hall, with the main doors on the far end. The doors set in the short passage yielded nothing but utility closets.

The question Bolan asked himself was simple—if the Russians had Rachel Logan in the house, where was she located? They needed to question her about two things—the location of her husband and the information he had hidden away. Bolan didn't fool himself into believing they would inquire in a gentlemanly manner. The fact she was a woman would have no effect on them—most likely the opposite. Rachel's femininity would be used against her. Bolan tried not to dwell on what they might do to her, but he was powerless to wipe images from his mind of former victims, some who had been friends. He had seen the things men were capable of doing to female captives. He would move heaven and earth to prevent them being visited upon Rachel Logan.

Bolan reached the end of the passage. The entrance hall spread out in front of him, with doors to the left and right, and a wooden stairway to the upper floor. He picked up the sound of heavy bootsteps coming from his left. A stocky figure, SMG slung over his shoulder, emerged from an archway. The man carried a steaming mug in his right hand, but he allowed it to drop as he saw Bolan's black-clad figure and clawed for the SMG. The mug was still falling when Bolan hit the guy with a short burst from the suppressed P90, the silent slugs ripping into the guard's torso. The man fell back, his face expressing shock. Despite his severe wounds he managed to yell a loud warning.

"Intruder."

Bolan knew enough Russian to recognize the word, and any thoughts of a quiet approach vanished.

The wounded man, on his knees, made another try for his weapon. Bolan's second burst ended that, spinning the man across the floor to slump against the wall, leaving a blood trail in his wake.

The response to the sentry's warning yell was fast and noisy. Bolan heard the thump of boots from the floor above, as two armed figures appeared at the head of the stairs. He dropped to one knee, angling the muzzle of the P90 and raked the area with solid fire. The two armed men were no more than three steps down when Bolan's spread caught them, 5.7 mm slugs thudding into flesh and breaking some bone in the process. One flopped back and stayed where he was. The other man dropped, slid down a couple of steps, then turned over and fell the rest of the way, doing more damage to his already bleeding body. The click of a door made Bolan turn and he faced another armed figure, sleeves rolled high on his brawny arms. The man snatched at an auto pistol tucked into his pants. His mistake had been to leave the weapon there before stepping through the door. Bolan triggered the P90, his long burst stitching the guy from stomach to throat. One of the 5.7 mm slugs ripped through his body to sever his spinal cord and he dropped to the floor and lay motionless.

Raised voices informed Bolan he was still under pressure. He tried to make out what was being said, but the distance lowered the level of speech. In essence, he was going to have to take on more of Koretski's shooters.

A fleeting thought—*was the man himself in the house?*

Maybe even the guy he'd just dropped?

Bolan threw a swift look at the downed man. He saw a short-necked, shaven-headed individual. No, not Koretski. The Russian boss was a tall, athletic man, with a head of thick blond hair.

The stutter of a full-on SMG burst through the Executioner's thought. He had been scanning his surroundings and registered a new shooter emerging from one of the closed doors. This guard came running, shouting wildly as he confronted the big American, his own P90, without a suppressor, jacking out loosely aimed shots that scored the tiled floor. The slugs hit with vicious snaps of sound, splintering the tiles and flying off at angles. Bolan felt something sear his right upper arm, tearing through the close weave of his black-suit before scoring his flesh. Bolan held his weapon firmly, tracked the shooter and put him down with a couple of bursts that turned the guy's knees to a bloody mush, bone and fragments of flesh exploding from the wounds. The man's yelling turned to screams as he collapsed to his knees, screaming even more when his knees slammed to the floor. For a moment his eyes met Bolan's and he had a brief glimpse of pitiless blue before Bolan's follow-up burst took his face apart and cored in to blow out the back of his skull in a moment of scalding agony.

Bolan came fully upright. He could feel warm blood streaming down his arm from the wound there. He dropped his gaze and checked the P90's magazine. He could see he was below halfway through the fifty shots. Still enough to be going on with before he needed to bring the MP-5 into play.

He realized a heavy silence had fallen over the house—no sounds of additional shooters. Unless any survivors had decided on a silent approach. He made a 360-degree check of the hall and the landing of the upper floor.

Nothing.

Perhaps the personnel in the house had been reduced because Koretski's main team was still out looking for Ray Logan. Bolan abandoned the theories. No point wasting time wondering.

He looked down at the man who had faced him from the room on his right. The double doors were only partly open, light spilling out from the room. Bolan moved on silent feet until he was able to peer through the gap between the doors.

He picked up on labored breathing. Not harsh like a man, softer, but betraying agitation.

Rachel?

Bolan toed open the closest half of the doors. It swung in and revealed a well-furnished room. Thick curtains drawn to shut out the night. Chairs and furniture had been pushed back to leave a wide circle of carpet. Two people stood in the exposed area.

One of them was Rachel Logan. Her arms and hands were held limply at her sides. She had been stripped naked. She stared at Bolan, eyes wide and moist with tears. There was a large, inflamed bruise on her left cheek, the discoloration already spreading to her eye which was swollen almost shut. Blood ran from the side of her mouth. An open gash plumped her lower lip. Bolan saw, too, bruises over her ribs. It took a great deal of control to stop himself from rushing forward to her aid.

He was prevented from doing anything because of the second person in the room. Medium height, lean and with a shaved skull. He had sunken cheeks above his thin mouth, and sharp eyes that were fixed squarely on Bolan. He wore a neat suit, tie and immaculate shirt. He had a slim-bladed knife touching Rachel's throat. Already a thin line of blood had run down her smooth flesh where the tip of the blade had pricked the skin.

Bolan knew who the man was.

Vigo Stone.

Kendal's running dog. The one they called The Enforcer. The cold killer who had slaughtered Marty Keegan and left his tortured body for his fellow cops to discover.

And here he was to implement his brutal technique on Rachel. Bolan, attracted by something shining against the light, glanced to the side. On a low table, resting on an unrolled towel, were Stone's tools. The scalpels and the pincers. Cruel steel instruments ready to be used on Rachel's vulnerable flesh.

"You've noticed," Stone said. "Nice collection." His tone altered, became harsh. "From the lack of resistance out there it looks like you took down all of Koretski's home boys. I told him to leave more. Now get rid of the arsenal, Cooper. Everything. If you try to screw around with me I'll cut the bitch's throat. You know I will. Your call."

"Don't…don't listen to him, Cooper," Rachel said. Her voice was hoarse, close to a whisper.

"Oh, I think he will. Look what he went through to get you out of that forest. Cooper, the senator was pissed at the way you took out his best people. All those dead bodies littering the countryside. He's not pleased. And Koretski is *slightly* annoyed, too."

"I'm all cut up about that."

"You might live to regret that phrase," Stone said. "Now get rid of the weapons."

Bolan shed his armaments and combat harness and dropped them on an armchair nearby. The Tanto knife was last.

"Now move away. We wouldn't want you doing anything foolish like trying to go for one of them, would we?"

Bolan sidestepped well clear of the armchair.

"You showing up, Cooper, has made things difficult. Or easier. Depends on how you look at it," Stone said. "I tie you up and let you watch. *Or* I tie the bitch up and work on you. I don't think she'll be able to stomach that long before she tells me what I need to know. Win-win for me either way. What do you think?"

"I think you're sick, Stone."

Stone smiled. "I wouldn't be in this line of work if I wasn't. Believe me, Cooper, that's the truth."

"I can understand that."

"For God's sake, Stone, do *something*," Rachel snapped. "Just stop talking. Listening to you makes me want to throw up."

"Feisty, isn't she?" Stone taunted. "Makes me figure it will be a shame to cut her up. Truth is I'm getting used to her butt pressing against me the way it is. Be a shame to give that up. But business is business."

Bolan saw the knife move fractionally from Rachel's throat as Stone's concentration wavered.

He also saw the color that flooded her cheeks. Saw muscles tense in her naked body and he knew she was about to do something.

Rachel jerked her head to one side, away from the threat of the knife. At the same time she pulled herself out of Stone's grip around her slim waist. Her strong body turned about as she swiveled on one foot, right arm swinging in a powerful roundhouse punch that connected with Stone's left cheek. It landed with enough force to make him step back, but not before his knife hand lashed out at her. Rachel gave a shocked gasp as the keen blade sliced across her shoulder, opening a long gash that began to bleed.

In that hectic moment Bolan dug his heels into the thick carpet and powered forward, his blacksuited body closing the gap before Stone had a chance to gather himself. Bolan slammed into the man and they were both catapulted across the room, crashing into a table, rolling across it and dropping to the floor on the other side. As they hit the floor Stone grunted, Bolan's weight holding him down.

The knife. Get the damn knife.

Bolan saw the blade rise and snapped out his left hand, fingers reaching to grip Stone's hand. He gripped the wrist, closing his strong fingers and twisted hard. Stone struggled, body writhing beneath Bolan's. The killer was lean but there was a lot of toned muscle there. His appearance was deceptive. Bolan maintained his grip, increasing his twisting motion. He saw the determined gleam in Stone's eyes. The guy was not going to quit easily, despite feeling the bones in his wrist start to grate as Bolan's action continued. Stone made to add his free hand to his right in order to overcome Bolan's grip, then apparently changed his mind and pounded his fist down at Bolan's face, clipping the Executioner's cheek. Bolan's head rocked from the blow and he felt flesh tear, blood start to course down his face. Stone grunted with the effort, drew back his arm to follow up with a second blow. Bolan had expected this and gathered himself, pushing up off the floor and throwing Stone off balance. Stone rolled free, jerking his knife hand clear of Bolan's grip. As the hit man pushed to his feet Bolan followed suit and they faced each other across a few empty feet of space. With a sneer on his face, Stone formed into a slight crouch, the blade held forward, still and deadly. There was no fancy waving of the knife, no suggestion to Bolan which way the man was going to move. Bolan stayed motionless himself, his eyes on the knife, watching and waiting for an opening. He knew that when his time came the window of opportunity would be small and would close with speed.

Stone came in fast, his knife aimed at Bolan's torso, intended for a deep cut that would rip into the Executioner's intestines. Bolan didn't attempt to stop the blade with his hands. He launched an unexpected leg sweep that arced round and hammered his opponent's knife wrist, catching it on the inside. Bolan's boot thudded home, Stone gasped at the intense pain as wrist bones were snapped. The knife spun from his fingers. It was still in midair when Bolan's other leg swept round and caught Stone in the ribs. He staggered from the impact. Before the man had time to recover Bolan stepped in. His left hand grasped the front of Stone's jacket, pulling him upright and placing him directly in line with Bolan. The Executioner's bunched fist slammed into Stone's face repeatedly, drawing blood and crushing his lips. The killer's cheek and eye caught more punches, his resistance starting to weaken under Bolan's relentless assault. A final blow sent Stone stumbling backward as Bolan let go of his jacket. Unable to stop himself Stone crashed into a glass-fronted display cabinet standing against the wall, the wood spacers snapping and thin glass splintering as Stone struck it, showering him with glittering shards. He hung upright for long seconds, then swayed forward, his face a bloody, ruined mask of blood and torn flesh. He might have stepped forward to confront Bolan if…

If the unexpected, thunderous crackle of auto fire had not filled the room. Stone caught the intense burst of fire in his torso and chest, the burning impact of the 9 mm slugs searing through his body, a number exploding through his back, the force of the sustained volley driving him back into the shattered cabinet before he dropped to the floor, blood soaking through his expensive suit and creeping out from beneath his ravaged body.

The Executioner turned.

Rachel had picked up the MP-5 that Bolan had been forced to put aside. She cradled the SMG in her slim hands, face taut with the anger she had expended, breasts rising and falling with agitation. Her trigger finger was still pulling back as if she expected the weapon to fire again. Bolan crossed to her and laid his big hands over the MP-5, easing it from her grip.

"You got him," he said softly. "He won't hurt you any more. Let it go, Rachel."

She stared at him for long moments before releasing her grip on the weapon, stepping back.

"He had that coming. He got off easy," she said. "I wish I could…"

She suddenly became aware of the thin knife cut in her shoulder. Blood was still oozing from the wound, running down her naked body. Bolan examined it. He slid his Tanto from its sheath and checked the heavy drapes covering the windows. He yanked one aside and found the thinner lining cloth on the other side. Using the Tanto he cut strips from the liner. He wadded a section and handed it to Rachel to press against the wound. On the other side of the room he spotted a drinks cabinet. He found bottles of vodka on the shelf. He took one and removed the cap.

"Sit down," he said.

Rachel watched as he soaked another wad of cloth with the clear liquid.

"What?" she asked as he stood over her.

"You like vodka?" he asked.

"Not really."

"Well, you're going to hate it now," Bolan said, and moved so quickly she had no time to react. He lifted her hand from the knife cut and pressed the vodka-soaked cloth against it, holding it firmly in place.

"Sweet Jesus," Rachel gasped, eyes widening as the raw vodka seeped into the wound. She snatched at Bolan's wrist, trying to remove it, but his strength was greater. Tears rose in her eyes as he pushed her hard against the chair back so she was unable to move. She understood what he was doing, but saw no reason to enjoy it. Biting back against the burning sensation she concentrated on something else. "Is Tommy safe? Cooper, is he okay?"

"Tommy is safe," Bolan said. "Probably back with Ray by

now. You'll be able to see him soon." He eased the soaked pad from her shoulder, checking the gash. The bleeding had slowed. He applied a fresh pad, then used more of the cloth to form a bandage that held it in place, winding it over her shoulder, under her arm, then securing it.

Rachel steadied her breathing, watching as he turned aside, crossing to retrieve her clothes from where they had been thrown to the floor. He handed them to her. Rachel held them, frowning until realization hit her.

"Oh," she murmured, then began to pull them on.

Bolan left her to it. He treated the score mark on his arm with another vodka-soaked pad, easily handling the expected sting, and then bound it with more of the cloth. The soft pulse of pain reminded him he was still alive and capable. He reloaded his MP-5, then picked up the Beretta and his knife. He spotted Rachel's Colt Commander on a desk at the far side of the room and brought it to her after checking the magazine. She glanced up from lacing her boots.

"Thanks," she said, on her feet. She took the pistol and tucked it behind her belt. "Shouldn't we be getting out of here? Koretski and his people could be back any time."

"You know where he went?"

"No. I just overheard him say he needed to push on with the deal."

Her eyes strayed to the blood-sodden body of Vigo Stone. Bolan noticed the involuntary shudder that coursed through her body. A delayed reaction to what she had done.

"Rachel, you okay?" he asked, his tone gentle.

"I've never killed anyone before," she said. "I mean how do…I…"

"Live with it?" Bolan sensed her uncertainty. "You did what was needed to survive. So that Tommy still has his mother. Do you think for one second Stone would have left you alive once he got what he wanted?"

She shook her head slowly. "I still…"

"You ended his life. You did it because you had a choice. It came down to him or you. Rachel, I'm not making light of this, but you did the world a favor. Stone won't be making anyone else suffer the way he did Marty Keegan. The way he would have made you suffer. Remember that and it might ease the pain."

"I know you're right, Matt, but it's a responsibility I'm stuck with now."

Bolan accepted that as an end to the debate and turned Rachel to the door. Conscious of the possible return of Koretski and company, he hurried her back through the house the way he'd entered. They paused at the door and Bolan released the bolts, easing the door open and peering into the shadows. He heard nothing but the sounds of the night. Saw no movement.

"Let's go," he said. "Stay close."

They made for the perimeter wall Bolan had used to breach the estate. He'd had no time to search for the electronic controls inside the house, so they took the easiest route out. He boosted Rachel up onto the wall and watched her drop out of sight on the far side. He hauled himself up, rolling across the top and dropped to the ground.

Bolan led Rachel along the side of the road, then into the thick bushes where he had left his SUV. He slid the keys from the pocket in his blacksuit and unlocked the vehicle. Rachel climbed in. Bolan opened the driver's door, unslinging his MP-5 and dropping it on the floor beside him as he settled in his seat. He hit the start button and eased the big Chevy out of cover and onto the blacktop. He left the lights off until they had driven a good quarter mile from the Russian house.

"Koretski is going to go crazy when he finds out what you've done," Rachel said. "He has a hell of a temper."

"Good," Bolan said. "If he lets his emotions get the better of him maybe he'll lose some judgment. That's when people make their mistakes. I like to be around when that kind of thing happens."

"You read people pretty well, Matt Cooper. And you play on their weaknesses. Isn't that what they call strategy?"

Bolan shrugged. "Works for me, whatever it's called. I

don't have the privilege of superior numbers, so I need to even the odds as much as I can."

"I still can't figure out exactly who, or what you are, Matt. I'm just grateful you came into our lives at this moment in time."

Bolan refrained from answering and Rachel didn't push the matter. He concentrated on driving, pushing the big SUV along the dark road at a solid speed. He only spoke once then, to inform her there was a first-aid box under her seat if she wanted to clean up the injuries to her face. Rachel drew it out and placed it on her lap, opening the lid and checking the contents. There was a square mirror fixed to the inside of the lid and when she caught a glimpse of her bruised and bloodied face it was a shock. She did what she could to clean herself up and applied ointment to her lips and cheek. She was still hurting from the blows to her ribs, and the knife cut in her shoulder stung wildly. The more she became aware of her sustained injuries, the more she resolved not to grieve for too long over her action against Vigo Stone. But she had a feeling that might turn out to be a short-lived resistance. Somewhere along the line she would realize her involvement in the death of another human being—despite Stone being a corrupt and soulless excuse for a man.

Some while later when Bolan glanced across he saw she had drifted into a restless sleep, her body's natural remedy for helping to heal. In Rachel's case that would be twofold—physical and mental recovery. Her body would recover far more quickly than her mind. The inner scars would be with her for some time. Bolan figured she would pull through. Rachel Logan had a strong personality, as well as a tenacious fighting spirit.

His only worry at the moment was the fact that she might need to rely on all those qualities before they were out of trouble.

21

"This time he has gone too far," Koretski ranted. He raised his arms and gestured at the bodies laid out in the hall. "This man, Cooper, has to die. He comes here. Kills my good men and runs away with the Logan woman." He turned and lashed out at the bloody corpse of Vigo Stone. "And Kendal sends in his paid killer to interrogate her without even asking my permission. He lectured *me* about interfering and then does this."

"At least you have the last laugh," one of his men said. "His supposed *top man* is dead. So much for these American hard men."

Koretski spun around on the man. "You think it's funny, Karel?"

Karel took a startled step back, face darkening with embarrassment. "I only meant…"

After a moment Koretski's features lightened and a smile curled his lips. "Actually," he said, "it does have a touch of irony. This man, Stone, was supposed to scare everyone. A heartless psychopath. The bogeyman to terrify us all. Look at him now. He wasn't so tough after all, huh? Not when he faced this Cooper. Now there is a man we should be wary of. He *is* good. So good he doesn't need to go around shouting about it. A man like that is worthy of respect." He laughed briefly. "Of course, I want him dead, too."

Yevgeny Epremov, second in command to Koretski, appeared. He hurried to his boss. The expression on his face told the Russian he had good news.

"We have him. The tracking device we planted in the woman's clothing is working. It came online a few minutes ago. They are heading south. Our calculations tell us they have at least an hour's start."

"All right, you heard that," Koretski told his crew. "Get moving. I want Cooper and the Logan woman retaken. Just remember the woman has to stay alive. Cut that bastard Cooper into little pieces if you want, but bring her back here still breathing."

Koretski followed Epremov to the room that served as a communication center. Epremov prided himself on his electronics setup. As they stood behind the man operating the system, Epremov showed Koretski the monitor that displayed the readout from the tracking program. It showed a moving signal superimposed on a scrolling map.

"This Cooper is no fool," Epremov said. "He stays inside the speed limits so as not to attract attention from any law enforcement. It means we have a better chance of catching up to him."

"Advise our people to be careful, too," Koretski said. "It would be unfortunate if *they* were pulled over and the local police found they are carrying weapons."

Epremov spoke to the tech and he relayed the instructions to the vehicles already leaving the grounds and taking up pursuit.

"I worry about Kendal," Epremov said. "I'm not sure I trust his judgment."

"And I didn't have to prompt you one little bit," Koretski said. "You worked it out yourself. I don't trust him, either. The man is arrogant. Everyone around him believes the sun shines from his ass. They hang on his words as if they are pronouncements from heaven. But the man has no grace. He snaps his fingers and expects it all to drop in his lap. Yev, he truly imagines he is doing me a big favor through this deal. *Doing me a favor.* Then again, he is about to make us a lot of money. So we will have to put up with him for a while longer." He tapped the tech on the shoulder. "Get me Kendal on the phone. I will take it in my office." As he turned to leave he said, "Yev, have the dead moved and dealt with. Get the place cleaned up. And keep me updated about Cooper and the woman."

Koretski returned to his office, a comparatively smaller room than most of the others. The Russian had never exhibited any signs of affectation. All he needed to command his organization was a desk and chair, a computer terminal and telephone. He was thinking about Senator Kendal and his ostentatious surroundings. The man really did display his wealth and power with a vulgar pleasure. As he sat behind his desk Koretski's phone rang. He picked it up and at that moment he remembered the news he had for Kendal. It almost made up for the invasion of his house by the man named Cooper.

"Make this brief, Maxim. I'm a busy man."

"As you wish. You sent your mad dog to interrogate the Logan woman while I was away. Not very polite, Tyrone. That said, don't forget it was my people who caught her."

"Fine, Maxim. We both bend the rules to suit our purpose. I thought Stone could make her talk far quicker than your people. Look how he got the information from Keegan."

"Keegan is dead. We need the woman alive."

"Stone can do that. Let me talk to him."

Koretski was unable to resist holding back the smile on his lips. "I can't do that, Tyrone."

"Why the hell not?"

"Vigo Stone is dead. The American, Cooper, hit my place while I was still on my way back. He took down my in-house crew. Killed Stone in the process, and drove away with the Logan woman. It seems we are all still being plagued by this fucking loose cannon."

The silence that followed Koretski's statement stretched. He could hear Kendal's heavy breathing on the other end of the line. For once the erudite senator appeared lost for words.

"Where are they now?" Kendal asked, his tone almost polite.

"On the road. With my people in pursuit. I had an electronic bug planted in the woman's clothing before she was sent for interrogation. Simple foresight that has paid off. Seeing as how she has proven to be an elusive character recently, I decided it would cost nothing to implement some precaution. Cooper has taken her from us but we know exactly where they are and I'm hoping to have her back within a short time. Now, Tyrone, are you going to be angry with me again? Or have we both learned a lesson in trust?"

"All right, Maxim, point taken. I think we are both being driven by this Logan problem. We can't forget the importance of getting our hands on that information, regardless of anything else." The senator took a breath then said, "Just to let you in on the latest development in Seattle, Captain Fitch, my police contact, and the two officers working with him, were found handcuffed together in a deserted building. It seems they were tricked into believing I had sent for them and Cooper overpowered the cops. The son of a bitch even rang to leave me a message about them. Made it clear he had been talking to them."

"He's a force to be reckoned with," Koretski said. "The sooner we remove him the better. But I say that with respect for the man. He has proven himself on more than one occasion. To *our* cost."

"He compromised my dealings with Fitch and his team," Kendal said. "I was forced to make certain none of them could be arrested if Cooper passed their names to some federal agency."

"Do I take that to mean Fitch and company will be unable to give away any incriminating evidence?"

"Exactly," Kendal said. "If any of them were placed in the position of saving themselves at our expense I'm sure they would have done so willingly. So they were silenced."

"Cleaning house is a necessary requirement."

"Which brings us back to Logan. The prime mover in this whole affair. His death would make me a happy man, so we do need to get our hands on the information he has secreted—or his wife. I'm still convinced she is the key to this. Find her and we should be able to locate that data."

"Then we should do this as a two-pronged exercise," Koretski said. "You concentrate on finding Logan and I will keep my people on his wife and this damned man Cooper."

22

They made a short stop at the side of the road so Bolan could change from his blacksuit back into civilian clothing as light began to invade the darkness. Then at first light they made a second stop at an isolated gas station that looked to be the only place of habitation along the high-country road. There was a house in back of the station and a tow truck parked alongside a dusty 4x4.

When Bolan had finished topping up the Suburban's tank he went inside to pay, saw that there was a merchandising section and stocked up on bottled water and a handful of cereal bars. Bolan spotted a coffee machine in one corner and purchased paper cups of steaming black brew. He paid for the gas and the other items and made his way back to the car.

Behind the gas station and across the road, heavily forested terrain stretched as far as the eye could see. In the far distance he could make out high peaks, some with a show of snow clinging to the tops. The thin breeze slicing down from the higher country had a fresh chill to it.

Bolan tapped on Rachel's door and she roused sleepily. She opened the door and he handed her the paper sack of goods and one of the cups of coffee.

"Is that really coffee I smell?"

"That's what it said on the machine. I can't guarantee the quality, so don't get too excited."

Bolan walked around to his door, climbed in and started the engine. They sat for a few minutes, sipping the hot coffee.

It wasn't the best Bolan had ever tasted, but it was also far from the worst. He wedged his cup in the holder and eased the Chevy back onto the road, picking up speed.

"Thanks for letting me sleep," Rachel said. "I really needed it. Hey, why not let me take over so you can rest?"

"I'm fine," Bolan said. He glanced at her. "I am, Rachel. I don't want you disturbing that shoulder wound in case it starts to bleed again."

"Okay." She peered at the satnav screen. "Where are we, by the way?"

"That's us," Bolan said. "The yellow triangle moving along that strip of highway. Apart from that I'm not too sure at the moment."

She gave a soft laugh. "My hero. Are we lost, Mr. Cooper?"

"Not exactly," Bolan said. "I'm just trying to put some distance between us and our hostile Russian buddies."

"Do you think they'll be coming after us?"

Bolan nodded. He knew Rachel Logan enough to tell her the truth. He was not going to insult her intelligence by pretending everything was fine.

"Koretski isn't the kind to let things go. Not after what I did back there. And he'll still want to get his hands on you again."

"I understand that. We'll just have to deny him that pleasure, won't we?"

Less than twenty minutes later, as Bolan followed a wide curve in the winding road, he spotted two vehicles less than a quarter mile back. He maintained his speed, watching in the side mirror, and from the way the two were edging close he guessed unwanted company was on the way. His fears were realized when he saw a figure lean out of the passenger window on the lead car, the outline of an SMG cradled in his hands.

"Rachel, check your seat belt," he said calmly.

Out of the corner of his eye he saw her do exactly that, then reach down and ease her Colt from her belt. Practiced hands checked the weapon, then laid it across her thighs. She moved her head so she was able to see the rearview mirror.

"I see two cars. Any chance they might just be travelling the same road?"

"Look to the passenger side of the lead vehicle. Guy leaning out. I don't think that's a Kodak Brownie in his hands."

"Hell, no, it's a…"

She didn't complete the sentence.

The exposed man opened fire. Flame winked from the muzzle of the SMG, sending a stream of slugs that crackled along the blacktop on her side of the SUV.

"You think he wants us to stop?" Rachel asked, the sarcasm clear in her tone.

"They want you alive," Bolan reminded her, "so that was just to let us know."

Rachel powered down her window, twisted herself round in her seat. She leaned out and aimed the Colt Commander, loosing off a trio of well-spaced shots at the pursuit car as it closed the gap. She scored a single hit out of the three. Her final round tore a ragged gouge in the car's hood. The car braked violently, tires squealing. The car swerved until the driver brought it back under control. The second car had to maneuver quickly to avoid rear-ending the lead vehicle.

"Now I *really* understand what Ray meant when he said not to get you mad when you have a gun in your hand."

"You think? That was lousy shooting. One hit out of three. I need to catch up on my range practice."

Bolan was studying the pair of vehicles. They were hanging back a little, obviously taking a warning from Rachel's aggressive shooting. But that wouldn't last for long. They would be under orders from Koretski to stop Bolan and retrieve Rachel. And the Russian would not be expecting them to return empty-handed. So one way or another, Bolan could expect a further response from them.

"Rachel, they want *you* alive. That might give us an edge. I have no intention of letting them take you, so when it happens I'll be shooting to kill. I want you to understand that."

"You'll get no complaints from me," she said. "These people have done nothing but threaten our lives from the moment Ray got the goods on them. He's been shot. Our son has been forced into hiding and then made to go on the run. It hasn't been my best few days, either. So you do what you have to do, Matt Cooper, and we'll worry about the consequences later."

Bolan reached to pick up his MP-5. He hung it around his neck so it would be ready for a fast retrieval.

The lead pursuit car powered up close. Bolan saw it grow larger in his mirror. The crackle of auto fire could be heard above the roar of engines. Slugs embedded in the rear panel. And then the tailgate window shattered, glass fragments imploding.

"The other one is trying to move in," Rachel said. "My side."

Bolan scanned the mirrors and identified the second chase car as it powered by, accelerating along the opposite lane. More gunfire came from the lead car, slugs thudding into the rear of the SUV. He threw a glance out of Rachel's window and saw the nose of the other car as it drew level with her door.

"Hang on," he said and yanked on the wheel.

The heavy bulk of the big Chevy struck the car just ahead of the front wheel, the solid impact pushing the vehicle to one side. Bolan held on tight, letting the maneuver gather momentum. Tires burned the road, smoke streaming as the car lost its grip. Bolan kept his foot on the gas, not letting up, and without warning the sliding car struck the rocky edge of the road. Metal screeched. Broken fragments flew into the air. Bolan caught a blurred glimpse of the driver wrestling with a steering wheel that was not responding. The front of the car rose as it hit a large chunk of rock edging the road. Bolan quickly spun his wheel and took the Chevy away from the stricken car as it dropped again, the front dipping, gouging the road. Then it rolled, starting to flip over on its side. Sheer weight and forward motion increased the spin and the car hung in the air for seconds before crashing down on its roof. Sparks flew from beneath the overturned bulk as the car continued forward. The driver of the other car had to swerve violently to avoid being hit and the rear end of his vehicle slid on protesting tires before he pulled it back under control. The upturned car began to spin on its roof, shedding pieces, and then one of the rear doors sprang open and a flailing body was flung out onto the road. Arms and legs thrashed as the victim tumbled along the blacktop, clothing and flesh shredded by contact with the coarse tarmac.

In his mirror Bolan saw the lead car right itself, starting to speed up and regain its close contact with the SUV. He reached down and freed his seat belt.

"Matt?"

"Stay down below the window line," he said.

Bolan eased off the gas, hit the brake and sent the Chevy into a long skid, off the road and along the dusty strip. He released the door catch as the SUV slithered to a stop, kicking it wide and exiting the car. He hit the ground, crouching, and moved quickly along the side of the SUV, never once taking his eyes off the lead car as it braked, turning broadside on as it slowed. He was ready as the vehicle came to a stop partway on the verge, and brought the MP-5 into play, triggering a long burst that blew 9 mm slugs through the windshield and the side windows. His relentless volley continued as Bolan moved forward, raking the Russians' car unmercifully. The slugs found human targets as well as steel and glass. Bolan was ready as the MP-5 clicked on empty, his fingers ejecting the spent magazine and replenishing the weapon in a practiced move. The SMG crackled again as he closed in on the car, firing down into the passenger compartment. The far-side rear door was pushed open and a bloodied figure tumbled to the ground. Bolan skirted the front of the car, catching the guy as he staggered upright, shoulder and face bloody where he had been hit. The Russian carried a customized AK-74 and he was already raising the weapon when Bolan confronted him, tracked in the MP-5 and hit the guy in the torso and chest with a hot burst. The Russian went backward, losing his balance and hit the ground hard.

Bolan checked out the interior. The three men inside were dead. There were scattered weapons among the blood and shattered window glass.

Looking back up the road Bolan studied the overturned car. Nothing moved around or inside the wreck. Smoke was trailing from beneath the crumpled hood and he saw the first flicker of flame showing.

Rachel was standing beside the SUV, inspecting the damage to the bodywork where Bolan had used the car as a battering ram.

"We still drivable?" he asked.

She looked at him, then over his shoulder at the two cars. "More than they are," she said.

"I warned you," Bolan said.

"I know and it had to be done. Matt, how did they find us so easily?"

Bolan had been wondering about that himself. He knew no one had tampered with the SUV because of time and the fact he had it hidden before he went inside Koretski's house. That only left one alternative.

"They must have planted a bug on you," he said. "After they took your clothes away."

"I don't understand. They already had me prisoner. They were going to try and force me to tell them where the data had been hidden. So why plant a bug?"

"Insurance. In case you got away and ran. Someone was hedging his bets. Let's say you did escape. Where would you go? Back to Ray."

"But I still don't know where he is."

"They might not have known that. So they gambled. Koretski is no fool. He was playing the odds. Taking no chances."

It took them almost twenty minutes to locate the miniature transmitter clipped inside the flap that covered the zip of Rachel's jeans. It was a small, button-shaped device that had sharp prongs on the underside and it had been hooked into the denim.

"All they had to do once it came online was watch our progress on a monitor screen and relay the information to the chase cars."

"That's just sneaky," Rachel said and Bolan couldn't help but grin.

Bolan threw the bug away and turned back to the SUV. "Let's go," he said.

"Hey, you don't think they might have planted any more?" Rachel asked. "I'm damned if I'm taking my clothes off any more. It was bad enough back there with that Stone guy leering at me."

"I don't think so," Bolan said.

They were pulling back onto the road when the overturned car blossomed into flame, sending a pall of thick smoke into the clear air.

23

"That's it," Grisov said. "The SUV with the damaged front corner. Plate number the same."

His partner, Tajik, took out his sat phone and made contact with home base. When Koretski came on the line Tajik relayed the information.

"What are they doing?" the Russian asked.

"It looks like they are going into a café. Yes. They have gone inside. What do you want us to do?"

"For now, just watch them. There isn't much else we can do while they are in the town. Keep a close eye on them. Wait until they are somewhere alone. Away from any witnesses. Just keep me informed. And do not lose them. Help is on the way. It will be there in minutes."

Tajik put away the phone. "He doesn't expect much," he said. "We have to wait until we can take them when they are alone."

"Two cars followed them along a deserted road and *still* couldn't stop them," Grisov said. "Are we expected to work a miracle here?"

Tajik shrugged. "If we hadn't received that call from Berin on his car phone we wouldn't have been able to identify that damned SUV. He must have known things were going wrong. I could hear shooting in the background. Now the matter is in our hands."

"Are you trying to cheer me up? If that's your intention it isn't working."

Tajik slipped his hand inside the leather jacket he wore, easing his fingers around the butt of the auto pistol in its shoulder rig. The move was to give *himself* a little assurance—it didn't work.

"YOU THINK PEOPLE are looking at us?" Rachel asked.

"Why would they?"

"We have enough bruises between us to suggest I'm a battered wife and you're a falling-down drunk. And you're checking everyone out like you expect trouble any minute. *I* think we look suspicious."

She hunched against the corner of the booth they had taken by the window after entering the café.

"Get you anything?" the waitress asked when she came to their table.

"Two coffees," Bolan said, looking the woman directly in the eyes. "And two of the specials off the board."

The waitress stared at Rachel, who abruptly turned to stare back at the woman. "Sorry," she said. "I thought you were going to say something."

The waitress backed off and went to the counter to place the order.

Bolan grinned. "I thought *you* were going to snap her head off."

"Did I look that angry?" Rachel asked Bolan.

Their coffee arrived—hot and black and fresh. It helped. The food came on large plates, necessary because of the large portions. Steak, mashed potatoes and greens, and hot biscuits, served with rich gravy.

"These two steaks represent almost a whole cow," Rachel said.

They ate, aware of how hungry they actually were. For a while conversation dried up until Rachel noticed Bolan kept staring out the window.

"What is it, Matt?"

"Two guys across the street. Outside the shoe store. They were around when we drove in and they're still there."

"Locals watching the world go by?"

"Those clothes they're wearing look a little out of place for a small town like this. They look like Armani models."

Rachel resisted the urge to stare. "Is this one of those intuitive moments you seem to have on a regular basis?"

"You could say that."

"Great. Just as I'm enjoying my first decent meal in days."

"They're not going to do anything as long as we're in a crowd. So eat your steak."

"Well, at least I'll die on a full stomach," she grumbled.

Bolan watched a uniformed figure crossing the street in their direction. He wore a full belt and holster around his solid waist, a baton on his other hip, the microphone of his comset clipped to his shirt, a badge over his left pocket, and a wide-brimmed hat on his head. The man looked to be in his late forties, tall and with a good physique. He stepped up onto the sidewalk and pushed open the café door, removing his hat as he entered. Bolan watched the lawman's reflection in the window and saw him cross to the counter and speak to the waitress. She nodded in the direction of their booth, then poured a mug of coffee for the man. The lawman left his hat on the counter, turned and walked across the café. He approached steadily, his right hand well clear of his holstered sidearm, his coffee in his left hand. He stopped at the table.

"Afternoon, folks," he said pleasantly.

"Sheriff," Bolan said.

"Mind if I join you for a moment." It was less a request and more of an assertion—he wasn't about to be refused. He slid onto the seat alongside Rachel. "Ma'am." Polite. Nonaggressive.

"You have some civic-minded people in your town," Bolan said. "Concerned about the condition of the lady's face. She called and you responded."

The sheriff sipped at the hot coffee. "They make a nice brew in here." He placed the mug on the table. "Name's Tetrow. I like to think we have a nice attitude here. Braxton's Halt is a small town—everyone knows each other. So newcomers tend to stand out and get noticed. Now, Nan, the waitress who called me, *was* concerned."

"And you being the town peacekeeper came to see for yourself," Rachel said.

"Yes, ma'am, that's correct."

"Sheriff Tetrow," Bolan said, "I'm going to reach into my back pocket. I have something I need to show you."

Tetrow nodded briefly, his eyes fixed on Bolan. He watched the wallet emerge, saw it flip open and saw the plastic ID card Bolan carried for just this kind of situation. It identified one Matt Cooper as an agent of the Justice Department. The phone number, if called, would connect with Stony Man Farm, where Bolan would be verified as genuine. He took out the card and slid it across the table so that Tetrow could study it in detail.

Bolan unzipped his leather jacket and showed the sheriff he was carrying. The lawman took a long look at the holstered Beretta auto pistol, then looked up at Bolan.

"They let you fellers carry nonregulation sidearms?" he asked.

"Kind of goes with the nonregulation operations."

Bolan closed his jacket. He took a sidelong glance out the window. The pair of observers were still in place.

"I've been keeping my eye on that pair myself," Tetrow said without looking away from Bolan. "Like I said, newcomers get noticed."

"They're watching *us*," Bolan said. "My guess is waiting to catch us alone."

"This to do with the lady?"

"Rachel Logan. Her husband is a cop in Seattle. He worked undercover and gathered evidence certain parties don't want airing. He was on the run before I became involved. Got himself shot and wounded." Bolan glanced at Rachel.

"Go ahead," she said.

"Since then we've been trying to keep one step ahead of trouble."

"What he's playing down is the fact that he's put his life on the line to keep me and my son alive. We drove down from the Cascades area after he rescued me from a nasty situation. But we were followed by some kind of hit team and nearly didn't make it."

"I did hear on the radio about some kind of fracas on the road some sixty miles back. A burned-out wreck and another with a mess of dead bodies in it. That to do with you?"

Bolan nodded. "They forced the issue. It was them or us."

"These people do that to your face, Mrs. Logan?"

Rachel said, "Yes. They want me to tell them where my husband is and where his evidence is hidden."

"And there I was thinking another quiet day in town," Tetrow said. "Cooper, what can I do to help?"

"Rachel needs some medical attention. She has a knife wound to her shoulder and some bad bruising to her ribs. There a doctor in town?"

"I'll be fine," Rachel said.

Bolan and Tetrow ignored her.

"Ganging up now," she said.

"Doc Malachi's office is across the street. Finish your meal and I'll walk you over there."

Tetrow picked up his mug and returned to the counter where he spoke to the waitress. Nan picked up the coffeepot and followed Tetrow back to the table.

"I owe you folks an apology," she said. "Seems I read the signs wrong."

"You keep reading those signs," Bolan said. "Not enough people who care these days."

"Goes for me, too, Nan," Rachel said. "And that steak was the best I've had in a long time."

"Honey, you visit any time you want."

"Talking of visitors," Tetrow said, "what about our boys over there?"

"They've seen us talking to the local law," Bolan said. "That might be stirring up trouble. You got any backup?"

"Not on hand," the sheriff said. "Both my deputies are out

on patrol. We cover the county and it spreads us somewhat thin at times. Today being one of those times."

TAJIK WAS BACK ON THE PHONE to Koretski.

"Cooper and the woman are in the café talking to the local lawman. He joined them a little while ago. I don't like it, boss. Maybe they will call in reinforcements to take the cop's wife away. If that happens and she talks to them, we lose our advantage."

"Then she becomes a liability instead of an asset," Koretski said. He didn't even pause to think about it. "That must not be allowed to happen. Kill her. Kill them both."

"How soon can we expect backup?"

"The helicopter will be with you in moments according to the pilot. He can see you."

Grisov said, "They are coming out of the café."

"We have to move, boss. They will be out on the street in a moment. They may have already called in for assistance. We have to move."

"Do it," Koretski said.

Grisov crossed to their parked car and popped the trunk, reaching inside to get at the weapons they carried there. He hauled out a pair of loaded AK-47s, each holding taped double magazines, and as Tajik dropped his phone into his pocket Grisov tossed him one of the assault rifles.

BOLAN SAW THE COMING ATTACK as he followed Tetrow out of the café. The sheriff had picked up on the Russians arming themselves and he yelled a warning to Bolan. As he un-leathered his 93-R Bolan half-turned, his left hand grasping Rachel's shoulder. He forced her back inside the café with an order for her to drop to the floor.

"Everybody down," Bolan added for the benefit of the rest of the customers, then turned his attention to the Russians powering across the street, AK-47s coming to firing positions.

Bolan leveled the Beretta, gripped double-handed, and

tracked the closest guy. He was already squeezing back on the trigger when the familiar, hard crackle of AK-47 auto fire filled the air. The first burst of 7.62 mm bullets scorched the air above Bolan's head, slamming into the awning above the café windows, tearing at the wood. Bolan heard the *chunk* of slugs hammering into the timber.

Then his Beretta fired, a 3-round burst delivered with measured accuracy. The 9 mm slugs caught the running target in the chest, dropping him to his knees. The AK-47 kept firing, jacking more slugs into the surface of the street, before the guy went facedown. Bolan delivered a follow-up burst that took the shooter out of the action.

More auto fire sounded. Slugs thudded into the parked car Sheriff Tetrow was using for cover. A rear tire blew out as it took hits. Light covers exploded.

"Son of a bitch," Tetrow exclaimed, then scooted toward the front of the vehicle, leaning across the hood to exchange fire with the advancing shooter.

The Russian, Tajik, was burning through his magazine, raking the café frontage, hitting the large windows and reducing them to glittering shards.

Tetrow triggered a second round of shots and saw the shooter stumble. By this time Bolan had his own weapon on the guy and hit Tajik with a double 3-round burst that ravaged the man's upper chest and throat. Tajik stumbled on for a few steps, blood coursing from his lacerated throat, then slammed facedown on the street, the Kalashnikov slipping from his fingers.

The rattle of gunfire faded, only to be replaced by the distinctive *thwack* of spinning rotor blades.

Bolan, stepping down from the café sidewalk, picked up the sound, glanced up and saw the dark bulk of a chopper dropping rapidly to street level, armed figures already leaning out from the open side doors.

24

Bolan acted even as the thought entered his head. He was moving forward, reaching for one of the dropped AK-47s, snatching it up and turning in toward the descending helicopter.

One of the armed men hanging from the open hatch triggered his own auto rifle. Badly aimed due to the moving aircraft, the 7.62 mm slugs blew pockmarks in the street.

Bolan dropped to one knee and shouldered the AK-47. He triggered a number of bursts at both the shooter and the chopper's front canopy where the pilot sat. The shooter jerked back inside the helicopter, clutching at his shoulder where a single slug found its mark, and the pilot saw his plastic canopy star as slugs struck home. Bolan kept up his strikes, muzzle turning back and forth. A final, long burst and the Plexiglas canopy imploded. The pilot jerked back, letting go of the controls as his face was torn by plastic fragments, eyes blinded as they were pierced. The chopper, no more than a few feet above the street, dropped heavily, skids buckling under the dead weight. There was a moment of confusion before armed figures burst from both sides of the passenger compartment. They hit the street and began to scatter, using parked cars and trucks for cover.

Bolan counted six of them.

Sheriff Tetrow broke cover and sprinted across the street to snatch up the other dropped AK-47. He continued on to take cover behind a dusty truck, returning fire from the disgorged helicopter crew.

The heavy sound of auto fire drowned out any other sound.

Bolan spotted a figure edging along the side of a parked Ford, his Kalashnikov clutched across his chest. The Executioner set his weapon on the man and hit him with a single shot that cored in between his eyes and tore out the back of his skull. The gunman pitched sideways, jerking awkwardly as he lived out his final moments.

Bolan heard shouted commands in Russian. Someone was giving orders to the crew, urging them to locate the *woman* and finish her. He hoped Rachel couldn't hear what was being said, couldn't understand the language.

A pained scream came as Tetrow tracked one of the less cautious Russians and put him down. Bolan saw the man stumble into view, hunched over from a gut shot. The moment he was fully exposed Tetrow hit him again, a burst ripping into the man's upper chest, spinning him off his feet, bloody spray erupting from a severed artery.

Skirting the line of vehicles angled in at the sidewalk, Bolan made a fast run, outflanking the Russians, emerging on a level with two of the crew. His quick move had left them without a target. They became aware of Bolan in the final seconds, twisting around as he rose from cover and triggered his AK-47, punching 7.62 mm slugs into them. The pair caught the full burn of Bolan's fire, bodies jerking under the impact of close-up hits. Punctured clothing and flesh blossomed with red as they tumbled back into the street, the high-velocity Soviet projectiles doing maximum damage in the minimum of time.

More fire from across the street alerted Bolan and he headed in that direction, making a swift magazine exchange as he moved, utilizing the double-taped configuration. With a full load Bolan raised the Kalashnikov and planted a burst between the shoulders of the Russian who had stepped up to fire at Tetrow, even as the sheriff engaged the remaining shooter. Bolan's target lurched forward as 7.62 mm slugs blew out through his ribs, taking chunks of heart and lungs with them. He dropped without a sound, seconds before Tetrow's shooter fell.

"We done here, Cooper?" Tetrow asked. He gripped the AK-47 like he was expecting more action. He absently reached up to wipe at the streak of blood on his left cheek where something had clipped the flesh. "I ask you something, son? Just what is it the lady's husband uncovered that is so damned important to these people?"

"I've been asking myself the same thing, Sheriff, ever since this whole thing blew up in my face."

"Well, it's got me real curious."

"Let's go and see if anyone got hurt in the café," Bolan said.

Rachel stood in the café door. "No one hurt," she said. "But the place is a mess." She touched Bolan's arm. "You okay?"

"I'm fine."

"Matt, I'm beginning to feel as if I bring problems wherever I go."

"None of this is your fault, Rachel. It's all down to Senator Kendal and his Russian partner. And I'm going to bring it to a close." He saw Tetrow on his radio comset, calling in his deputies and caught the man's eye. "I'm taking Rachel over to the doc, then I need to make some calls."

As he led Rachel across the street, steering her away from the carnage, she pulled up short.

"It's time I told you where Ray's data is hidden," she said. "I wouldn't trust anyone else right now. You should go and get it. Bring it in so we can put a stop to all this. Maybe then I can get back to my husband and my son. It's been a hell of a ride, Matt Cooper, but I just want to be a wife and mom again."

Bolan pushed open the door to the doctor's office.

"Sounds like a reasonable request," he said.

TETROW HAD ORDERED his deputies to drop whatever they were doing and to return to town. He called in further help from other law agencies, shaking his head as he leaned against his desk in the sheriff's department.

"I'll be filling out paperwork for the next month," he said. "If I was a vindictive man, Cooper, I'd be asking why the hell couldn't you have driven right through here and stopped off at the next town."

"Let me make my call," Bolan said, "and I'll see if we can smooth some of this over for you."

"Nine bodies and a helicopter *bang* in the middle of the main street? How in hell do you smooth that over?"

The office door opened and Nan came in. She was carrying a coffeepot and a couple of mugs. "Figured you boys could use some of this," she said. "How you doing? That's a damn fool question seeing as how you just came through a firefight." She poured coffee, then said, "So, how're you doing?"

"We'll survive," Bolan said.

"And Rachel?"

"The doc treated her. He gave her something to help her relax and right now she's asleep."

"Best thing for her," Tetrow said. "Maybe I'll go ask the doc to treat me and I can lie down and sleep."

Nan laughed. "Don't let him fool you, Cooper. Our sheriff is tough as boot leather."

"Grateful for the coffee, Nan," Tetrow said as a way of getting her to leave. She took the hint, placed the pot on the desk, and left, quietly closing the door. "Cooper, you going to be making official, confidential calls? I can step out if you want."

"No need."

Bolan used the sat phone to make his call to Stony Man Farm. While he waited for his connection to go through the safety protocols he took a drink of Nan's coffee. He saw Tetrow settle in his chair behind his desk. The sheriff stared out the office window and Bolan could almost read the man's mind as he reviewed the sudden and violent events that had disrupted the peace and quiet of his town. The memory would linger.

"Striker?" Hal Brognola's tone was tinged with worry. "You okay? More to the point, what the hell is going on and where are you?"

The conversation for the next few minutes was one-sided, with Bolan relating his version of recent events. He completed his report with details of the incident in Braxton's Halt.

"You and Rachel Logan are okay?"

"Few scrapes and bruises. Rachel is resting at the doctor's office. I need some help out here to get this town back to normal. Have a word with Leo over at Justice. His Federal Task Force clout should be able to cut through the red tape."

Brognola grumbled something about having to clean up another fine mess. But Bolan knew the big Fed would do it.

"Striker, how is it you can be driving through a quiet town and next thing get yourself involved in a mess like this?"

"What can I say, Hal, it's a gift."

"Okay. You've told me where Ray Logan is. His son is with him. And you have Rachel Logan under your protection. Now how about letting me in on this damned evidence that everyone seems to be busting a gut to get hold of."

"To be honest, Hal, I don't have much to tell you. Something to do with Senator Kendal's association with this Koretski guy."

"A Russian gangster and a U.S. senator in the same mix. That's a recipe for one hell of a shit storm, Striker."

"Let's not forget what's been happening to the Logan family. And a murdered Seattle cop. And the two people killed at that store. All they did was get in the way of Kendal's and Koretski's hired guns. Too high a cost, Hal."

"We don't forget anything, Striker. What's your next move?"

"See that Rachel gets back to her family. Then I go and retrieve Ray Logan's evidence. And whatever you can dig up on the senator would be helpful."

"See what I can get. You might find Kendal still trying to get his hands on this evidence, too."

"I'm counting on that, Hal."

Bolan's simple remark was enough. The words hit home and Brognola understood the implication—the mission was far from over.

The Executioner was still out there.

25

"You up to talking?" Bolan asked Ray Logan.

"After seeing my wife and son safe and protected, Cooper, nothing can stop me now."

Bolan sat down beside Logan's bed. He needed answers but he didn't want to tire the man. Logan looked weak, his face pale and drawn. His recovery was going to be slow.

"Ray, we haven't had a chance to go into too much detail over why Kendal and Koretski are so desperate to stop you from talking and airing the evidence you gathered."

"Things did get hairy once you picked me up," Logan admitted. "I was kind of out of it for a while and by the time I came back you were gone."

"Then wasn't the time. But now it is time," Bolan said.

"Well, it took some figuring out, but I finally realized what they were up to." He fell silent then, staring out the window, gathering his thoughts. Bolan realized just how much effort even this small conversation was taking.

"Ray, if this is too much…"

Logan shook his head. "No, it's okay," he said, voice reduced to a dry whisper. "It's oil, Matt. A massive field Koretski found out about from one of his own field engineers. Under the water along the Alaskan coast. Once developed it's going to be worth billions of dollars, and Koretski and Kendal want to control it all. They clamped down on reports and surveys, and they had a number of people killed to prevent disclosure. It's all in my data. Names. Dates. Kendal has been using his influence to make sure everything swings his way. Bribery. Blackmail. That man is unstoppable. Partnership with a Russian criminal makes him one hell of an opponent."

"That's enough to go on," Bolan said. "I'll recover the data and we'll shut them down for good."

"Rachel tell you where she planted it?"

Bolan nodded. "Yes. She hid it well."

"She's some lady," Logan whispered. "Did I thank you for looking out for her and Tommy?"

"More than once."

Logan was drifting, eyes closing as his energy level dropped. He didn't notice when Bolan quietly left the room.

There were two Stony Man Blacksuits stationed in the Madsen house. Bolan had a quiet word with them before he left. No one would get into Logan's room, apart from his family and Doc Madsen and his wife. The Blacksuits answered only to SOG authority—Brognola and Bolan. The Logan family were in safe hands. Rachel and Tommy were sleeping, resting up after the events of the past few days.

In his SUV Bolan linked up with Stony Man Farm again. This mission, originating as a solo endeavor as far as Bolan was concerned, had expanded into something bigger and before the Executioner made his moves against Kendal and Koretski, he needed to understand exactly what they were doing. The whole affair had taken on a wider aspect: the involvement of three cops from Logan's Seattle department who had been found executed after Bolan had left them; the murder of Marty Keegan, Logan's longtime friend; the execution of Sarah and Arthur Kenner—two completely innocent citizens. Bolan's rescue of Rachel Logan had culminated in the open, pitched battle in Braxton's Halt. All these occurrences were a result of Ray Logan's undercover assignment exposing the Kendal-Koretski alliance.

With Logan's revelation about a massive oil find, Bolan finally had a motive for the desired cover-up. The Executioner was under no illusions. Greed and the need for power were old bedmates. It wouldn't be the first time the primal lust for control of some unexpected discovery brought out men's worst sides.

"Tell me what you've found out about Senator Tyrone Kendal," Bolan said.

"With what Hal was able to get, plus what we've dug up, we now have a clearer picture of the man. You want the full biography, or the *Reader's Digest* version?" Kurtzman said.

"Short and to the point, Bear."

"A bully and full of his own self-importance. Apparently you should never turn your back on him, even if you're in a crowded room in broad daylight. He truly believes personal aggrandizement was created for him alone. He gets away with a lot because he's extremely wealthy and has powerful connections. Interestingly, though he's protected, the man is still not making real friends. And it seems a lot of his acquaintances have been turning their backs on him lately. He's been up to too many tricky dealings it appears. Nothing anyone can take him to task over, but the word from the Hill is he's getting walked around whenever he shows up. And I did get it on good authority that he's used up most of the favors people owed him."

"He's keeping bad company, Bear."

"The gossip is that he runs in very dubious circles. No proof, of course, but I did pick up a whisper about him having a relationship with one Maxim Koretski. Moving on to Koretski—he seems to be one of those new Russian entrepreneurs. Has his hand in all kinds of schemes—made a fortune in property, oil and shipping. But the *unofficial* word is Koretski has links to the Russian underworld."

"Bear, where do you get all this from?"

"I spent most of my adult life in politics, and I lived inside the Washington Beltway. You don't exist in that bubble without gaining all kinds of information. I may be out of the daily grind, but I keep my ear to the ground and I still have my sources. At my age, Matt, I need something to keep life interesting."

"I have information, which needs confirming, that Kendal and Koretski are partnering in some oil-prospecting deal. You come across anything about this?"

"Nothing yet."

"It appears this deal is being kept under wraps because Kendal and Koretski are vying to gain full control. Looks like a covert, backdoor operation," Bolan explained. "Listen, if you get something else that might be useful, you know how to get me?"

"You got it, Striker." And with that, the call ended.

BOLAN'S CALL FROM Kurtzman came faster than he had been expecting. The Stony Man Farm cyber expert had interesting news for Bolan.

"I had a long conversation with a police contact inside Moscow's Organized Crime Department. He did some poking around for me and came up with more on this oil business. He remembered a report about a private aircraft crashing, killing all four passengers on board and the pilot. It was flying back from Alaska. Nothing could be proved other than that the plane apparently developed engine failure over a desolate area. The flight manifest gave the names of the passengers. They were all involved in the oil industry. When I ran some in-depth checks on these people I found they worked for an oil commission based in Seattle. There was also mention of a company called *Nuevo Oil, Incorporated*. Small business. Been around for a few years. When I ran a search program, tracing back through company files and various layers, it emerged that the guy behind *Nuevo Oil* is none other than your Russian buddy, Maxim Koretski. He wanted to stay below the radar, but you can't hide from Uncle A. After the crash, all reports, surveys, etc., were lost, vanished, erased. It was like these guys and their assignment never existed. Seems there was a rumor about a big find, but the downer was it turned out to be just that—a rumor—and it all fizzled out after the deaths of those people in the plane crash."

"Ray Logan said his undercover assignment led him to a connection between Kendal and Koretski. He believes the senator is working in tandem with Koretski to bury any and all references to this oil find while they gain title and full control," Bolan said.

"Right now I have the team digging into Kendal's affiliations. He presents himself as a simple guy, working for the people. He supposedly stepped away from the family empire, handing over the reins to appointed board members. Be no surprise if somewhere down the line our honorable senator is still in control. He keeps it in the background but all the time he's still head honcho.

"My contact has his suspicions that Kendal has been forcing individuals in government to turn blind eyes to his behind-doors dealings. He smells bribery and blackmail in the mix. Kendal has a rep for using underhand tactics—extreme if necessary. Example—look at what he's done to Ray Logan and his family."

"I think Logan has him running scared," Bolan said. "If all the gathered evidence comes out, Kendal will be finished and so will his backdoor deal with Koretski. That's my next step. To retrieve that evidence so we can confront Kendal and company."

"They could still have people out there, Striker. People working on the assumption Rachel Logan took the evidence with her when she ran and hid it somewhere in the area."

"Thing is they would have guessed right and, yes, they could still be looking. I'll face that if it comes up."

"We'll keep on looking into Kendal's and Koretski's backgrounds," Kurtzman said. "I have a feeling we'll uncover all their sneaky dealings and connections. I'll keep you in the loop, Striker."

26

Bolan heard the movement of a number of bodies as Kendal's crew edged through the shrubbery around the secluded cabin. He was able to assess how many as they filtered across a clearing, then moved into the thicker trees, spreading as they went.

Okay, he had their head count. They moved quickly and not too quietly, each man scouting a different section. They likely figured they knew what they were doing, but the noise they made marked them as unused to this kind of environment.

As far as Bolan was concerned the men needed to be taken down quickly. He saw them as a viable threat so any actions he took had to be direct, utilizing time and effort to the best of his ability. He could not afford to be pulled into a drawn-out engagement. Letting himself be cornered would work for them, but would be fatal for Bolan.

He was back at the cabin where Rachel and her son had been hiding out in order to reclaim the evidence Rachel had concealed. It was his sole objective. On the other side of the coin the same thing applied to this armed crew. Their objective, for a different reason, was to gain the information in order to protect Senator Kendal and Maxim Koretski. If the pair got the evidence they would destroy it. Without it, Ray Logan's offensive would be weakened to the point where Kendal's lawyers would shut the cop down.

With Logan still recovering from his bullet wound and his

family under protective custody by Stony Man, it was down to Bolan. He had shouldered the responsibility without regret. Stepping in to help someone like Logan was no hardship for the Executioner. From day one of his ongoing war, Bolan had taken the side of the underdog. He saw good being abused by the predators—blood spilled in vain because many of those being attacked were not equipped to fight back. And it was that which attracted Bolan. He simply would not stand by and allow it to happen. He *could* not allow it to go unpunished. He hated the bully—the evil side of man that was expressed in senseless acts of violence, of taking away from the weak and the gentle. There needed to be a force to combat the baser side of humanity.

That force came in the black-clad figure of Bolan.

Never one to shirk his duty.

Never one to step away in the face of danger.

Bolan was one man, but a man of heightened abilities, who seldom thought of his own mortality. If he had, it might have taken away his edge. He understood his day might come, later rather than sooner, but gaining that understanding he was able to push it aside and operate on the premise that for as long as he could fight his war, he would.

And that was what he was doing on this day.

Bolan didn't miss the sudden rush of boots coming in from his right. He had been spotted.

He did not miss the hasty words as his would-be attacker pronounced that he had found the target, speaking into his comset to warn the rest of his crew. The man had cast aside the golden rule of combat by announcing his presence—he might as well have shouted out loud and beat it on a drum.

Bolan swiveled in the guard's direction, letting his SMG hang by its strap as he reached to unsheathe the black-handled Cold Steel Tanto knife he carried. As he turned his back to the thick knotted tangle of undergrowth, legs braced to support his low crouch, Bolan heard the rustle and crackle of the closing man. The guy may have caught a glimpse of the Executioner before his headlong rush, but in his haste he'd failed to securely pinpoint Bolan's position, so it was no hardship for the soldier to set himself. As the enemy lurched into sight Bolan reached out with the Tanto, pushed upright, and sank the chill length of steel into the man's throat, feeling little resistance. There was a low gurgle, the only sound the man made, then a slow trickle of blood that quickly became a steady stream as Bolan worked the knife across the throat, cutting deeper. A sigh of breath whispered from the ravaged throat as the man slipped to his knees, all reason gone, only the final seconds of life remaining as Bolan withdrew the blade, then made the killing cuts left and right, severing main arteries. As pumping blood surged forth, Bolan pulled back and the man fell facedown, his body riding out the spasms that shook it.

Bolan sank the Tanto into the soft earth to clean off excess blood before he sheathed it. He picked up the SMG the man had dropped, recognizing the configuration of the weapon.

FN P90, 5.7 mm, holding a 50-round top-loading, translucent, polymer magazine. He checked the weapon—it was loaded and cocked. He could use it. Fifty extra rounds.

"Where's Slick?" someone called. "Which way?"

This to Bolan's right.

And close.

"Over your way."

Bolan picked up the rattle of undergrowth. He moved to the edge of the thick tangle and peered through the hanging fronds. A wide-shouldered figure came into view, carrying a weapon similar to the one Bolan had just acquired.

He raised his own weapon and eased the muzzle through the hanging leaves, locking on to the man with wide shoulders. Bolan's finger stroked the trigger and the SMG stuttered briefly, the shots loud in the near silence. The target stopped in his tracks as Bolan's shots hammered into his chest. The man toppled back, lost in the undergrowth as he went down without a sound.

"Over here," another yelled, still failing to understand the concept of not revealing his position.

Bolan ranged in on the guy, caught him full-on and hammered him with a controlled burst that blew bloody spray from the exit wounds. The guard went to his knees, uttering low moans that fell to silence when Bolan put a final burst into his skull.

Someone opened fire, aiming at shadows, firing by reflex, fear, panic.

Bolan smiled tightly as he heard the slugs snapping through the undergrowth yards away. He caught the muzzle-flashes and used them as his firing point. His SMG jacked out a long burst and he heard a following cry of pain as the target caught the slugs in his midsection, doubling over in agony.

"Son of a bitch," someone shouted. "For Christ's sake, peg the bastard."

Bolan heard them coming, spotted shadowed figures as they converged on his location. He made three of them. He raised his weapon and let go with tight groups of shots, tracking the muzzle back and forth. Bolan held his position, using his shots well and saw figures stumble and fall, their bodies slamming hard to the ground. As the third guy dropped, Bolan stood upright, moving in and placing killing shots into them all. He discarded the empty SMG and unlimbered his MP-5.

He heard the comset of one of the dead crew still issuing muted commands. Bolan secured the unit and listened to the ranting words coming through the headset.

"No one left to answer," Bolan said into the microphone. "Next time try hiring a better quality dirt bag, not street trash."

"They come cheaper by the dozen," Eddie Bishop said. "And money is no object."

"I know who you work for. Here's your chance to walk away and tell the senator I'll be paying him a visit soon. Count it in days. And keep checking over your shoulder. One time I'm going to be there."

Bolan dropped the headset and crushed it under his boot,

then turned and melted deeper into the undergrowth and the close-growing timber. He picked up his pace, only checking the GPS unit a couple of times to fix his position. According to the coordinates he was close. He would be on his target within a couple more miles.

He reached a spot where he was able to pause and hear the distant sound of rushing water. That meant he *was* near the place. Rachel had told him he would hear the water before he saw it. Bolan followed the sound, and it increased as he moved toward it.

Behind him birds broke out of the trees, swirling, circling, disturbed by a presence. Bolan knew he was still being followed by the survivor of Kendal's crew. He kept going, letting the guy track him. The man was persistent. Carrying out his orders.

Orders to follow Bolan.

To allow him to locate the evidence, then to take it from him.

And to kill him.

Bolan was about to change those orders—in his own favor.

The man following Bolan was going to pay for his error. Bolan had given him the opportunity to back off. To walk to comparative safety. The man had declined that offer.

It would not be given a second time.

27

Eddie Bishop crouched in the cover of thick undergrowth, watching the man he knew as Cooper. He was staying well behind the black-clad figure, the recent deaths of his crew still vivid in his mind. Cooper was one hell of an opponent. A man would have to be a complete idiot not to take into account Cooper's skill and his survival instinct. Bishop figured this guy had to have some impressive combat experience behind him to have come through the various confrontations and still be alive. Even Koretski's so-called top men had fallen under Cooper's guns, and then the man had even visited Koretski's home base and taken out not only the Russians, but Senator Kendal's *killer dog* Stone.

Bishop had given an inner, silent cheer when he'd learned Stone was dead. A personal, albeit immature, feeling, but what the hell, he had never liked the man. He had, of course, kept his thoughts to himself when Kendal had called him in to reestablish him as head man in charge of the crew. It had been a hard task to maintain a dignified expression at the news, and Bishop had the feeling the senator knew exactly what he was thinking. He detected a gleam in Kendal's eyes that betrayed the man's inner imagining.

"It must be quite a blow, Eddie, to learn Mr. Stone is dead."

"I guess I'm still in shock, Senator," Bishop said. "This Cooper is a hard son of a bitch to take down. If Stone lost out to him…"

The senator quickly lost interest. "Yes, well, it happened, so we have to move on. The problem is still out there. Logan and his wife are where we don't seem to be able to get at them. But this evidence Logan gathered is still missing and anything that cop has to say still needs backing up with his evidence. Rachel Logan didn't have it with her when she was taken to Koretski's base. Stone was about to get her to talk when Cooper dropped in and fucked the whole deal. That tells me the evidence is still up for grabs and my instinct tells me she hid it while she was secreted at that cabin."

"You thinking she told Cooper? Gave him the location?"

"Out of a number of suggestions, it's the most likely unless we come up with anything else. But check out the facts. She was up in the wilderness for a while. Enough time for her to hide that evidence in a secure location. It's a wild place—a good place to hide something. Get a team together, Eddie, and get back out there. This Cooper character has been bucking the odds all the way down the line. First he brings the woman back to a safe place, then most likely reunites her with her husband and son. The next logical step is to recover the evidence. My guess is Cooper takes on the job. Let's do this, Eddie, and prove I'm not making another error in judgment."

BISHOP WAS NO FAN of the forest environment. His adult working life had been spent in urban jungles. Certainly not this green, leafy place, where the ground was soft underfoot with dead plants and the air had a slightly moldy odor. He was well out of his comfort zone, and that had applied to his team. The way Cooper had taken them all down could have been classed as embarrassing if it hadn't been tragic. Three of his longtime buddies dead in minutes once Cooper had them spotted. He had closed in with less effort than it took Bishop to open a bottle of Bud—one, two, three, and they were gone.

So here he was, Eddie Bishop, on his own and tracking a man who dispatched his opponents with ease. He crouched, staying low, letting Cooper get farther away. He had no way of telling whether Cooper had him spotted. The SMG Bishop was gripping was slick with sweat beneath his hands, and under his clothes his flesh was oozing perspiration, too. Bishop accepted he was not cut out for this kind of operation. But, he worked for the senator, and Kendal gave his orders with the expectation they would be carried out. Bishop was from the old school—you take a man's money, you see the job through, no matter what. Putting your life at risk came with the territory, and nobody lived forever. Money-wise the job paid well, very well. Senator Kendal understood the dangers and he made sure his operatives were looked after.

The hell of it was, all that money did little to make Bishop feel better in his current situation. If he caught a gut full of 9 mm slugs his bulging bank account was not going to do him any favors.

Bishop saw the blacksuited figure step over a rise and drop out of sight. He waited then pushed forward himself, the spot where Cooper had vanished fixed in his mind. As he plowed his way through the undergrowth, Bishop picked up the sound of rushing water. It came from somewhere ahead of where Cooper was trekking. Bishop increased his pace, cursing as he stumbled over exposed roots, stepped into water that had gathered in hollows. Something caught his cheek, stinging and leaving a bloody spot. He sleeved the irritation away. He felt the ground rising as he neared where Cooper had dropped out of sight. The sound of water rose to a higher pitch.

When he dropped to his knees, peering over the rise, hands pushing aside the tangled undergrowth, he realized the source of the noise.

A waterfall, dropping some twenty-five feet from a wide, rushing stream. It fell in a silver curtain to a large pool, bouncing off rocks worn smooth by the ceaseless volume of water. The far side of the pool emptied itself into a wider, slower-moving creek that meandered across a grassy meadow before curving out of sight through the verdant forest. Misty spray rose from the base of the waterfall. A spread of pale rocks littered the ground on the approach to the pool.

Cooper was standing motionless, looking out across the pool, his gaze centered on the fall of water. He held something in his left hand, checking a readout. And Bishop realized what it was—a tracking unit. An electronic gizmo that had led Cooper right to the spot where the Logan woman had stashed her husband's evidence. He wondered what it was.

A bug emitting a signal?

Or the coordinates for a GPS unit?

Whatever it was Cooper had followed the trace right here. Right to the evidence.

Bishop held back. He needed to wait until Cooper had the material in his hands. Then he could take it from the man. If he jumped too soon Bishop might still have difficulty laying his hands on the evidence. He would let Cooper bring it to *him*.

Just take your time, Eddie. Don't screw up now. Just think, when you walk in and present the senator with his package, he'll most likely hand you a million bucks in a brown paper bag.

Bishop pulled himself back to reality. *Quit the daydreaming,* he told himself. This was no fucking game. The guy down there was no fairy godmother. He'd chew him up and spit out the bones if Bishop lost his concentration. *So get a grip,* he ordered himself. Bishop glanced down at his P90, checking the weapon and convincing himself he had a full magazine.

When he looked up again Cooper had gone.

Vanished.

Disappeared as if he had never been there.

That was the moment Eddie Bishop felt the panic set in.

28

The feeling stayed with him. Bishop did not consider himself a coward. He had faced personal danger on many occasions. His chosen lifestyle meant he was often placed in such situations. So he took the risks and handled them as they came. This time was different. This man, Cooper, was like an unstoppable force. There was no other way to describe the guy. He was not reckless, despite facing and taking on huge odds. The man showed no fear, or if he was scared he didn't show it. His moves were calculated, his judgment sound. And he showed little mercy to anyone who stood against him, which, after being said, was another scary realization. Bishop fought the urge to turn around and walk away, to hell with Kendal and his orders. It would have been easy on a physical level. But Bishop had more respect for himself. Here he was, ready to face Cooper, knowing he was going to pit himself against the best he had ever faced, the man who had cut his way through Kendal's crew. Who had also taken on Koretski's Russians, and he understood the likelihood of defeat. Yet he pushed himself out of cover, searching for Cooper, and felt the rising buzz of personal danger far stronger than he had ever felt it before.

He scanned the area, searching for Cooper.

How had the guy moved so quickly? And where had he gone? He hadn't gone in Bishop's direction. If he had, they would have come face-to-face. That meant Cooper must have gone forward, across the slabs of rock circling the waterfall.

Bishop studied the falling curtain, the spray it created as it struck the pool. Was it concealing Cooper? At this very second he could be tracking Bishop, waiting for the right moment. Bishop didn't fool himself into believing Cooper would give him any leeway. The man would strike at any given moment.

Bishop dropped to his knees, using a chunk of rock as cover, aware he was too much of a target.

As he dragged himself behind the rock he heard the single shot, saw stone chips flying as the slug impacted. He felt stinging fragments bite his cheek. Blood stippled his flesh.

Son of a bitch almost had him.

Bishop leaned around the edge of the rock. From the angle of the shot it had to have come from behind the waterfall. There was nowhere else Cooper could have hidden.

Okay, hotshot, my turn.

Bishop triggered the P90 and raked the curtain of water with a long burst, tracking back and forth.

Then he moved, clearing cover and cutting to the side, taking himself around the edge of the pool and closer to the fall.

He opened fire a second time, placing his shots into the curtain of water, then flopped belly-down on the edge of the pool.

"I know you're in there, Cooper," he yelled. "Nowhere to go. I can keep you pinned as long as I need." Bishop had no idea how long that might be, but he had to maintain his persona. "Let's negotiate. You know what I'm here for. The senator wants that evidence you came back for. He's a powerful man. He can do you a lot of good. Give him what he wants and you can walk away a rich man."

Silence.

Bishop clicked in a fresh magazine.

"Cooper, it's a dead end where you are. I got you covered. Now there's a sat phone clipped to my belt. I can call the senator and he can send in a chopper loaded with armed men. Between the senator and Koretski, they can bring in a small army. Hell, some of those Russian boys *were* in the military. They know tricks I couldn't imagine. We can surround that pool and just sit it out, or you can walk out now, with the evidence, and we can end this. It's your choice, Cooper. You want to talk, or do I make that call? I'll make it easy. Let you think it over. Fifteen minutes, then I make the call. Fifteen minutes. Counting down, Cooper."

29

Bolan didn't like ultimatums. Mainly because they presented him with forced decisions, and forced decisions were never recommended. If he had been the type to buckle under pressure that would have been a secondary consideration. Bolan, however, reacted to scenarios with this kind of threat with his usual direct action. If Bishop figured Bolan would fold and hand over the evidence simply because his back was to the wall, then the Kendal hardman was in for a surprise.

The GPS coordinates had led him to the waterfall and the shallow cave formation behind it. It ran no more than ten feet deep. Crossing the smooth worn stones from the pool Bolan had flattened against the rock face, then moved quickly behind the falling water. He had turned on instinct to check his back trail and had seen the lone, armed figure appear at the edge of the pool. The surviving guy from Kendal's crew had made better time than Bolan had expected.

He had raised the MP-5 and triggered a shot at the moving figure, his slug too high. It clipped the rock where the guy was crouching and sent him into cover. Bolan accepted his shot had been hasty—a reaction to Bishop's sudden appearance. Firing through the curtain of water had deflected his aim enough to take his slug off target. And before Bolan had time to adjust for a second shot Bishop had opened up with a couple of rapid bursts. Slugs struck the rock face behind Bolan, forcing him to drop to a crouch. The snap of the slugs against the rock had been accompanied by the higher whine of ricochets, threatening a higher degree of hits. By sheer chance Bolan received only one strike as a flattened slug seared a gouge across his left shoulder. It made him aware of his precarious position as he clamped his hand over the stinging wound, feeling warm blood seeping through his blacksuit onto his fingers.

Then he picked up Bishop's shouted warning. His threat to call in reinforcements and his "generous" time-out to allow Bolan to consider his position.

Bolan had no intention of paying any attention to the threat. If Bishop had backup he was able to call in, it would take time. And Bolan had no worries on that score. Bishop might not realize it, but his own span of time was rapidly diminishing. Allowing Bolan a grace period only allowed the Executioner the opportunity to make his own play, regardless of the risk.

As the fifteen-minute period began, Bolan turned his attention to locating the concealed evidence, following Rachel Logan's instructions on where she had placed it. He moved to the rear of the shallow cave and found the spot easily. Moving a covering of loose stone fragments Bolan eased out the bulky package Rachel had placed there. He exposed the flat attaché case wrapped in a black plastic sheet she had bound in layers of duct tape. A smile edged his lips as he saw the amount of tape she had used. Her thoroughness would have put the creators of Egyptian mummies to shame. He made no attempt to open the packaging, instead leaving it wrapped in the plastic sheet and placing it aside.

His immediate concern was getting clear of the cave and dealing with Bishop. A frontal assault was not in Bolan's favor. There were too many variables in making a rush attack from behind the waterfall. Bishop had the area covered from his land-based position. He would be watching for any overt move.

Bolan's agile thought processes spun through a number of possibilities and he quickly discounted them, coming to the only one he decided had the best chance of working. Even that one had drawbacks, but he went with it, and once he had made his decision he acted on it.

He stripped off his combat harness and placed it at the back of the cave, along with his MP-5. He cleared his black-suit pockets of everything, including his sat phone, leaving him with just his sheathed Tanto knife and the Beretta 93-R, which he set for triple bursts and secured in the shoulder-rig holster.

Moving to the far side of the cave, away from Bishop's position, Bolan eased himself into the pool, fingers gripping the wet rock ledge. The water was cold—Bolan ignored it. He took a few minutes for deep breathing, filling and emptying his lungs before he filled them one last time, then lowered himself beneath the water, kicking to the bottom of the pool until he touched the stony floor. The depth of the pool ran to around ten feet. Above his head the surface of the pool was stippled by the falling water, covering Bolan's movement as he swam clear. He was counting on Bishop concentrating his gaze on the waterfall itself, not the rest of the pool.

Bolan's muscled legs and arms thrust him forward, across the pool. He turned his head and through the hazy depths he made out the far edge, where the ten feet was reduced to no more than a couple. He used the rough bed of the pool to pull himself forward, then turned in toward the shallower side. He had allowed himself at least twenty feet when he turned, seeing the daylight grow stronger as he moved in to the side. As the water became shallower, the image of the poolside became clearer and Bolan was able to see the outline of Bishop crouching behind his covering rock. Bolan's circuitous route had brought him around to Bishop's left side. The man was fully exposed—and well within range of the 93-R.

Bolan reached across and slid the auto pistol from its holster. He felt the bed of the pool under his boots and pushed up, water cascading from him as he cleared the surface.

As Bolan's blacksuited form erupted from the water it took a couple of seconds for Bishop to register the movement out the corner of his eye. He reacted, his body leaning back, the SMG swinging round in the arc that would bring it onto Bolan.

He was way behind.

Bolan fisted the Beretta in both hands, the muzzle settling on Bishop. The first triple burst cored in under Bishop's left arm, the impact moving the man's body so that the next three 9 mm slugs impacted against his chest. Bolan nudged the muzzle up a fraction, firing again. The trio of Parabellum slugs tore into Bishop's throat, severing flesh and muscle that flowered bright blood. Bishop fell back across the rock that had been protecting him, his finger belatedly squeezing back against the trigger of his SMG. The muzzle was still aimed out across the water and the burst harmlessly sprayed the surface of the pool.

Splayed out across the rock, his senses already fading, Bishop watched the figure of Bolan emerge from the pool, water shedding from the blacksuit, the big auto pistol in one hand.

"You...tricked...me..." Bishop husked through the blood spilling from his mouth. The taste of it was heavy, metallic, and with each of his shallow breaths it spurted thickly.

Bolan looked him in the eye. "No. I out-thought you is all," he said. Then Bishop moved for his SMG—but he was too slow. Bolan eased back on the Beretta's trigger, delivering his final triple burst. The top of Bishop's skull lifted under the impact and bloody bone and flesh flew free.

Bolan crossed to the waterfall, ducking behind the curtain of water. He geared up, retrieved the attaché case and emerged into the daylight again. He passed Bishop's body and paused to retrieve the man's dropped sat phone. Bolan checked the call list and saw that the man's last call had been to SK. It wasn't a big leap of the imagination to translate that. Bolan thumbed the call symbol and listened as the connection was made. The voice on the other end of the line was strong, authoritative.

"This better be good news, Bishop."

"Seeing as how I have that package you've been so desperate to get your hands on, Kendal, I don't believe that's the case."

"Who the... *Cooper?* Is that you?" The shock edged out of Kendal's voice. "That's *Senator* Kendal by the way."

"Not for much longer. Once this evidence is in the right hands your time is going to be up. You lose, Kendal. Your get-rich scheme is about to be laid out in the daylight for everybody to see. You and your Russian partner are finished."

"Fuck you, Cooper. My God, boy, you must be stupider than I imagined. You think I'm going to roll over and play dead? No damn way. I'll walk away from this and come out smiling. You have to understand who I am. Realize the influence I have. The people I control are so high up the ladder you wouldn't be able to see them on a clear day. Take me on, Cooper, and I'll squash you like the fucking cockroach you are."

"At least that makes it easier for me, Kendal," Bolan said. "Expect me to come calling on you and Koretski. You've done enough throwing your weight around. There are deaths to account for—time to pay the bill."

Bolan cut the call, turned and threw the phone into the water.

"House call on the way, Kendal. Executioner style."

30

Tyrone Kendal's vacation home was a split-level, ranch-style house in Teton County, fifteen miles from the small town of Choteau. The area was home to a number of ski lodges, the higher slopes providing access for the skiers who flocked to the area during the season. Kendal used the house when he needed to be away from the pressures of Washington and any other distractions. The house was isolated at the end of a two-mile private road leading in from the main highway, with the majestic sweep of snow-covered mountain peaks as a backdrop. Here Kendal could relax and let his excesses drain away.

But at the moment the peaceful ambience of his retreat was not working its magic. He had been there for four days, ensconced with his chief legal advisor and a five-man security detail, waiting for Koretski.

And he was not enjoying his enforced isolation. For the first time in a long time, he felt distinctly unsettled.

Secure in his home, surrounded by his armed bodyguards, Kendal was unable to shake off the feeling of unease. Since his brief conversation with the man named Cooper, there had been no follow-up. No sight nor sound from the man. Nothing about the supposed recovery of the evidence the Seattle cop, Logan, had gathered. The inactivity and the silence was a damn sight more unnerving than if Cooper had actually shown up.

Kendal attempted to fill the waiting time—because he

was convinced something was going to happen—by throwing himself into work. He'd also been having long discussions with his lawyer as they sought to build a strategy that would protect Kendal from any possible legal threats. Simon Daggett was a brilliant lawyer, almost worth the hefty fees he charged. His knowledge of law, the loopholes and the twists and turns, were meat and drink to the man. His law firm in Seattle had an enviable reputation—it charged high and achieved results. But Kendal didn't give a damn about any other successes—all he was worried about was his own skin. He had made that clear when he sent his private plane to bring Daggett to the Montana house, stressing that for the money he was paying, the lawyer should be considering moving in on a permanent basis.

They were seated in the spacious living room, a roaring log fire blazing in the deep stone hearth. Wide panoramic windows looking out across the valley over which the property stood filled two walls, with the snow-streaked slopes of the foothills beyond. To one side was the dining area, where a large dining table was currently occupied by Daggett's paperwork, with his assistant, Linda, an efficient and attractive young woman, seated and busy at her laptop.

"This Seattle police officer, as I see it, obtained much of his so-called evidence by unlawful means. He used a phone tap to record your conversations. Recorded and photographed details. And he gained access to your Seattle premises without any kind of legal warrant, thereby retrieving private information from your computer."

"You make it sound as if he's the criminal," Kendal said.

"Exactly," Daggett said. "We base our defense on that very thing. Invasion of privacy. Obtaining information illegally. I can build one hell of a case to get any prosecution simply thrown out of court."

"Simon, far be it from me to question your judgment, but all this cop has to do is offer his evidence to the media. What's to stop them from showing it on prime-time TV? Running a newspaper article?"

"We obtain a restraining order. It will stop any of the evidence from being shown or written about."

"And what if someone simply ignores that order and goes ahead? If that happens, I'm finished. Mud sticks, Simon. Once people get a whiff of anything it sticks."

"The D.A.'s office won't dare let that happen," Daggett's assistant said. She crossed to where Kendal and the lawyer were seated. "They know that anything out of step with the law will damage their case. It's happened too many times, so the D.A. will simply make everyone hold off until he can be one-hundred-and-one-percent sure he has a watertight case. Which gives us more time to build your defense."

"Linda is right, Tyrone. With the way things are these days the prosecution has to walk on eggs. Even a misspelled word in a document can get a case thrown out. They'll be going over everything a dozen times. Looking for the little things that I'll be waiting to jump on."

"The way they got their evidence will have them sweating about civil rights, abuse of procedures," Linda said. "The days of busting down doors and hassling suspects is long gone." She allowed herself a smile. "The law is on our side, Senator."

"Let's hope so," Kendal said.

One of his security crew rolled in a metal trolley holding a fresh pot of coffee and mugs. Kendal caught the man's eye and led him aside.

"Anything?"

"No, sir. Nothing. Two of the guys are on foot patrol, circling the house. Lucky for us the terrain is open and flat. No chance of anyone approaching without being seen."

"Has Koretski been in contact?"

"That was the other thing I came in for. He called a little while ago. He's on his way. Should be here in less than an hour."

"Thank you, Tony. Stay sharp now."

"You got it, Senator."

Leaving Daggett and Linda to their legal work, Kendal

took his mug of coffee and stood at the main window. Sky and mountains, the open green slopes running down past the house—it all looked so peaceful. And, as Tony had said, there was no way anyone could approach the house without being seen.

So why did he still feel vulnerable?

The answer came easily.

In three or four hours daylight would be gone.

It would be dark—and that made a difference.

Kendal picked up the house phone and called Tony.

"You did check the floodlights, Tony?"

"Yes, sir. All working. And the generator is secured."

"Fine."

Kendal put down the phone and returned to stare out the window.

"More coffee, Senator?"

It was Linda. She topped up his mug and glanced out of the window.

"It's beautiful up here," she said. "So different from the city. Quiet and peaceful."

And isolated, Kendal thought. *Out in the middle of nowhere. Just like Koretski's house up in the Cascades.*

"Son of a bitch, Cooper, where are you?"

"You say something, Tyrone?" Daggett asked.

"Just thinking out loud. It was nothing."

It had never occurred to Kendal that he might, one day, require security above and beyond a small crew of armed men. Like outside TV cameras, maybe with infrared to pick up any stray movement in the dark. The house had been his haven. It had been a place where he could sit back and simply enjoy the solitude—the eternal peace of the hills and mountains, away from Washington, away from his Seattle responsibilities. But all that had faded into the background. With the possible threat of prosecution and the greater threat from this man, Cooper, the house had become less of a home and more of a fortress. It made him aware that vast financial holdings and a high-ranking political position meant very little in a world where a lone man could end it all with the pull of a trigger.

Damn the man.

"Senator, Mr. Koretski's helicopter is coming in for a landing," Tony said, appearing in the living room.

"Thank you, Tony. See to his arrival. And help Simon and Linda gather their paperwork and make sure all their luggage is placed on board."

Daggett and his assistant were taking the helicopter back to Seattle to continue with the defense preparation. There was little more they could do at the house. Kendal had signed numerous documents, made statements. Next the work would take on a more complex set of procedures and Daggett would need his firm's experienced advisors to look into the D.A.'s charges.

"Thanks for your hospitality, Tyrone," Daggett said. "This is far from over. However the D.A. wants to play, there are weeks, maybe even months, of preparation ahead. The more time we can spend, the better our chances. You leave it in our hands. The D.A. wants a fight, he's going to get one."

Koretski walked into the room, nodding briefly to the lawyer and his assistant as they left. He crossed and shook Kendal's hand.

"Why so down in the mouth, *tovarich?* Things are looking up. I spoke with my people before we left. In a few days we will be able to sign the final papers, and then the field is ours. We will have joint ownership of that potential pot of gold. You and I are about to become even more wealthy than we already are."

Two solidly built Russians in well-fitting and expensive suits were standing across the rear of the room. Koretski noticed Kendal looking them over, his smile widening.

"I took what you said seriously. These are new men who came in from Moscow a few days ago. I have used them many times before."

"We both felt the same about all our other men," Kendal said dryly. "Cooper showed us just how *good* they were. I have three around the house and two outside. And do you know what, Max, I still don't feel safe."

"I admit this Cooper has dealt us some hard lessons, but do we fold our tents and crawl into the darkness? I think not, Tyrone. We continue to fight. This man cannot survive forever. Yes, I agree that he is skilled. Very adaptable. But he is still only one man. Human like you and I. It will take only one bullet to stop him." Koretski tapped the side of his head. "Cooper likes to play on our fears. To get inside our skulls. He wants us to be afraid of him. I will not let that happen." He clapped a hand on Kendal's shoulder. "Now, where do you keep your drink? That helicopter flight has left me thirsty."

Twenty minutes later the helicopter took off, taking Daggett and Linda away. Kendal watched it swoop over the house and recede into the distance. For a fleeting moment he wished he was on board himself, but then he wondered where he could go to get away from all his problems—and Cooper? Something inside whispered that no matter where he went the man would eventually show up.

Tony had gotten Koretski's two bodyguards settled. With their belongings squared away they were in the large kitchen eating. Kendal usually had a part-time staff when he was in residence, but this time he had not brought anyone in, so his own crew and Koretski's would be looking after their own needs. The chillers and fridges were well stocked with food, so feeding his visitors would not pose a problem.

Seated in front of the fire, with fresh drinks and coffee, food brought to them by Tony, Kendal and Koretski allowed themselves some time to discuss matters.

"Logan and his family have been hidden away where I can't find them," Kendal said. "Whoever Cooper works with, they have damned good security. We haven't even come close to locating them."

"Do you have people looking?"

"Damn right. I'm not giving up on that fucking cop. The trouble he's caused us I have an open-ended contract on him. Permanently open-ended. Someday, somewhere, he'll be found. When he is, the bastard is dead. So are his wife and kid."

"You do not forgive very easily, Tyrone."

"Damn right I don't. Nobody screws with Tyrone Kendal and walks away."

"I received word this morning that most of the heavy equipment has reached Seattle docks. It's housed in my warehouse complex. The drilling rig should dock in a day or so. My crew chief is assembling the manual crew. In a few days we will be ready to ship out and head for the field. Once the final contracts and permits have been issued we can move."

"Is Binder cooperating?"

Koretski laughed. "Oh, yes. He will make sure nothing official stands in our way. Every so often I send him photographs showing his relatives going about their daily business, just to remind him I have not forgotten what I promised."

The heat from the fire, the drink and food, lulled Kendal's senses. He began to relax a little as he and Koretski discussed what lay ahead. Time slipped by and it was only when Tony came into the room to switch on the lights that Kendal realized it was already getting dark outside. A light fall of snow was drifting down from the higher slopes. The outside floodlights came on, throwing a wide spread of illumination around the house. Kendal stood up and crossed to stand at the big window, watching the snow fall. The sky darkened rapidly and beyond the circle of light the landscape looked like a black void.

"Senator, I'm going to prepare the evening meal," Tony said. "Steaks be okay?"

Kendal nodded absently. "Sounds good, Tony. You go ahead. Are the men on standby?"

"Yes, sir. We have it all buttoned down."

"Thanks, Tony."

We have it all buttoned down.

Kendal stared out the window, clutching his tumbler of whiskey.

Would Cooper understand?

That the house was all buttoned down?

That voice was whispering inside Kendal's head again, and it was asking if Cooper *did* understand, would it make any difference?

Senator Tyrone Kendal found it hard to believe it would.

31

Bolan had been in place since midafternoon. He had seen the helicopter arrive and deliver Koretski and his security crew. He had watched as Kendal's lawyer and assistant boarded the helicopter and left. And from that moment it had become a waiting game. Bolan lay in a shallow depression that allowed him to watch the house and make his preparations. He was waiting for the darkness to drop. It would provide cover for him. It would allow him to choose his moment.

He had checked out the weather forecast and knew there would be a snowfall. It would reduce his field of vision, but would also do the same for Kendal's security crew. Bolan had already seen the two-man outside patrol. Kendal and Koretski would have the bulk of their people inside. Bolan's first strike would be against the armed patrol moving around the house when the floodlights came on as darkness fell. The wide cast of light, despite the snow, pinpointed the patrolling security men for him.

Bolan was clad warmly against the rapidly dropping temperature. The weatherproof suit, hooded, was worn over thermal clothing. Bolan was also wearing a pair of thermal gloves. He would remove them when he was ready to use the sniper rifle, protected for the moment inside the canvas bag that also held his other weapons.

The M-40 A-1 sniper rifle was an old model in some respects, but was still a dependable, rugged weapon. It had served the U.S. military for a long time. Chambered for

7.62 mm NATO rounds, the M-40 A-1 bolt action held five rounds in the integrated magazine. This wasn't the first time Bolan had carried the superbly accurate rifle. He knew it well, trusted it, and where matters of life and death were concerned he held it in great esteem. He screwed the bulky sound suppressor to the end of the threaded barrel. A Scout Sniper Day Scope was already fixed to the Picatinny rail, with the addition of a supplementary Simrad KN200 fitted to accommodate night vision.

Bolan judged the range to be less than 800 yards. He knew the M-40 A-1 had an effective range of 1,000 yards, expending a bullet at 2,550 feet per second. That gave him a formidable and deadly weapon. Despite the falling snow there was little wind motion, so he was not going to be presented with much in the way of drift. Bolan checked the weapon, worked the bolt to chamber the first round, then placed it on the canvas bag beside him while he made a similar check of his two handguns. The Beretta 93-R snug in its shoulder rig, and the big Israeli .357 Magnum Desert Eagle in a high-ride holster belted against his right hip. A Cold Steel Tanto knife was sheathed on his left side. Bolan wore a combat harness over his clothing, with extra magazines for both his hand guns. In one of the pouches were five-round clips of 7.62 mm loads for the M-40 A-1 in case he needed extra.

For Bolan this was going to be a fast in-and-out hit. That was how he had planned it. He had no desire to allow it to drag on. His intention was to deliver Executioner judgment on the men inside the house.

Both Kendal and Koretski were guilty on counts of murder. In Bolan's eyes that condemned them out of hand. The methods they used to intimidate and terrorize victims simply stacked up the chips.

In a session with Ray Logan and the Seattle D.A., Bolan had remained a silent observer. Bolan listened without saying a word as the D.A. spoke to Logan, and saw the pained expression in the cop's eyes as he began to accept the possibility that Tyrone Kendal might yet wriggle out from under the threat of prosecution. The D.A. made it clear the battle was far from over and every avenue would be explored, with the intention of bringing Kendal to justice.

Logan was shaking his head as he realized the sacrifice he and his family had made. The even greater one that had ended with Marty Keegan losing his life. The deaths of Arthur and Sarah Kenner at the store. The D.A. explained these were separate issues that had to be dealt with on their own merits. Kendal's behavior in regards to bribery and blackmail had to be handled with care because his defense team would be throwing counter pleas in Logan's direction.

When the D.A. had gone, assuring Logan his efforts would not go to waste, the cop had sunk back on his pillow, exhaustion creasing his face.

"That son of a bitch is going to walk," he said. "After everything he's done, he's going to walk away a free man. I put my life on the line and his lawyers will get him off. My wife, my son, went through hell because of that bastard. I lost my best friend on Kendal's orders. Innocent people died. Jesus, Cooper, maybe I should just throw in my shield and go get an easier job."

"No. You're a cop, Ray. A damn good one. I don't see you quitting."

Bolan walked to the door.

"You leaving, Cooper?"

"Something I need to do, Ray. But you rest easy. Kendal and his partner, Koretski, are not about to walk free. Take it from me, that's a given."

Which brought him here, to the snowy slopes of Montana, overlooking the senator's isolated safe house.

The current pair of security men, clad in cold-weather gear and carrying automatic weapons, made their predictable rounds, prowling the exterior of the house, checking the separate stone-built generator building standing some yards clear of the main property. They also inspected the pair of 4x4 SUVs parked alongside each other, standing close to the east side of the house.

He watched the activity of the guards.

With his ordnance checked and at hand, Bolan picked up the solid weight of the sniper rifle. He slipped off his right-hand glove, flexing his fingers to keep them supple. He studied the pacing guards, chose his first target and set himself. He was flat down, legs spread to brace himself. His left arm held the weight of the rifle, elbow supporting against the ground as he followed the movement of the man through the night scope. The full beam of the lights was projected away from the base of the house wall, so there were still shadows for Bolan to deal with. So he watched.

Waiting and waiting until he had the target where he wanted, then a slow, progressive easing back on the trigger. Feeling the pressure as the rifle's inner mechanism responded to his light touch.

Bolan felt the trigger snick back all the way. Felt the almost flat sound as the firing pin snapped forward.

Then the dulled sound of the shot. The solid kick of recoil against his shoulder.

Through the scope Bolan saw the target react as the 7.62 mm slug hit. The guard twisted, head spurting blood and brains and snapping to one side as the impact bounced him off the wall of the house. He went down on his knees, then toppled facedown on the ground, body jerking in dying spasms.

Bolan worked the bolt, ejecting the spent cartridge and jacking a second into the chamber. He pulled the rifle around to lock on to the second guy, watching him move in the direction of the rear of the building, unaware his partner was down.

As the guy rounded the corner he saw the first guard on the ground. He reacted fast, snapping his own weapon up, scanning the open ground beyond the house.

Bolan caught him full face on, the scope settling, steadying.

The M-40 A-1 bucked in Bolan's grip as he fired. The guard's head blew apart as the 7.62 mm slug cored in above his right eye. It blew out the back of his skull, spattering a glistening mess on the pale stone behind him. The guy stepped back, contacted the wall and slid down until he sat motionless in death. His auto weapon slipped from nerveless fingers. Then his bloody head dropped forward until his chin rested on his chest and his weight dragged him away from the wall.

Bolan saw none of this. With the two-man security detail out of the picture he was on his feet and moving downslope, heading for the house. He had placed the rifle back inside the canvas bag. Once he was inside, the need for a long-distance sniper weapon would be superfluous. His handguns were the only tools he would need for what lay ahead.

Bolan knew that Koretski had brought a two-man crew, but he hadn't been able to assess how many Senator Kendal would have around him. Knowing the man's propensity for excess it would probably at least equal, or even double the number the Russian had with him.

Bolan reached the house, skirting around the base until he located the rear door leading to the ground floor. He slid the big Desert Eagle from its holster and eased off the safety. Bolan checked the timber door—it opened at his touch. He eased through into a basement storage area, with a set of wooden steps leading to the house proper. A light showed beneath the door and, pausing briefly, Bolan picked up the murmur of voices. The smells of brewed coffee and cooking food told him he would be emerging into the kitchen area.

Bolan was about to open the door when it was done for him and he came face-to-face with a tall, broad-shouldered figure, sleeves rolled up and shirt open at the collar. The guy wore a shoulder rig holding a SIG P-226 and the moment he confronted Bolan he let out a warning yell and reached for the holstered auto pistol.

The Desert Eagle only moved a fraction, Bolan triggered a single .357 mm round that blasted its way through the man's torso, emerging through his spine and blowing a mushroom of blood and tissue across the kitchen.

As the stricken guard went back, Bolan went through the door, taking in the generous dimensions of the wood-and-stainless-steel kitchen. He saw at least three occupants, all dropping whatever they were holding and going for the weapons they carried. Shots rang out, slugs clanging against hanging utensils and shattering glass in cupboard doors.

Bolan had already taken a headlong dive to the tiled floor, rolling tight against a floor unit, feeling the shower of debris that filled the air from the initial fusillade of shots.

Men were shouting to each other. Shoes clattered on the tiles and shadows danced on the walls above where Bolan lay, his pistol searching for targets.

He saw a pair of shoes appear around the end of a unit and angled the Desert Eagle up, firing on instinct. His pair of .357 mm slugs ripped into the lower torso of his target and the man went down with a stunned cry, falling across the floor only a couple of feet from Bolan. The Executioner used another shot to the guy's skull, ending his suffering, then rolled away from where he was sprawled and gained his feet. He stayed below the level of the worktops, saw the head and shoulders of a figure. Bolan tracked him, then triggered the big handgun. The heavy slug tore into the man's left shoulder, the impact sending him reeling along the edge of the kitchen unit. The power of the .357 mm slug had shredded his muscle, severing a blood vessel, and the guy was bleeding massively. Blood spurted across the marble work surface, pooling dramatically. The hit man was losing blood quickly. He was effectively out of the game, his only interest in stopping his blood loss, a struggle he lost quickly.

Bolan had moved back, edging around the far end of the kitchen units, knowing that he needed to deal with the third guard before he became trapped in the kitchen. He could already hear distant calls from deeper in the house, and knew that the scant seconds that he had left would fall away with frightening speed.

The crack of a close shot pinpointed the third man. His bullet ripped a large chunk of marble from the work surface above Bolan's head. Having located the guy, Bolan crouch-walked around the end of the unit. He spotted his target far-ther along, at an intersection between two floor units. The man had his back to Bolan, appearing to be concentrating his attention on the far side of the kitchen. He only became aware of his error when the rising bulk of the Executioner flickered in the corner of his eye. He was already too late when he swung his gun arm around. Bolan's Desert Eagle spat flame twice and the slugs slammed into the base of the guard's skull, taking a large chunk of his face away as they emerged through his left cheek. The man crashed down hard on the kitchen floor, his blood spreading in a wide fan across the tiles.

Bolan made for the wide kitchen arch and ducked through, jerking to the left as he saw an armed figure lunging at him, SMG raised. The 9 mm slugs hammered the wall and wood frame of the opening. Plaster and wood splinters filled the air where Bolan had been a microsecond earlier. As Bolan lifted the Desert Eagle, he saw the shooter adjusting his aim. Double handed, Bolan triggered the Desert Eagle, pumping the remaining rounds from the weapon into the shooter. He saw the eruptions as the powerful slugs tore into the target's chest, throwing him backward.

Bolan's fingers plucked a fresh magazine from his harness as he ejected the empty one. He clicked it in, felt the slide snap into play, and was ready to fire again even as figures tumbled into view from the end of the passage leading to the front of the house. They came in a ragged bunch, too close, uncoordinated, and Bolan had the fleeting impression he was working a duck-shooting gallery as he fired shot after shot at the figures. His shots were on target, tearing into flesh, splin-tering bone and splashing walls and floor with fresh blood. The house echoed to the sound of gunfire, brass casings ring-ing against the tiled floor in a metallic rain.

Bolan was barely aware of exchanging the empty Desert Eagle for the tri-burst Beretta. And his body hardly registered the couple of hits he took in his side and hip.

Bodies slumped in the passage, bloody and torn, the reek of gunsmoke and the brassy stench of spilled blood filling the air.

As suddenly as it began, the savage confrontation ended. A man emitted a final gasp, air gusting from bloody lips as he sagged into a prone sprawl. The hard clatter of a weapon drooping from loose fingers alerted Bolan and he automatically reloaded his handguns, moving along the passage and stepping around the dead and the dying.

Three steps led into the large living room—plush and expensively furnished, a log fire burning in the open grate. Bolan went up the steps, leaning against the closest wall to support his body, his Desert Eagle in hand again. He could feel blood running down his left side where he had sustained bullet hits. It soaked his coverall. He would soon feel shock as the effects took over, but he had enough in him to complete his mission.

There were two men facing him.

The rugged figure of the Russian. And the suddenly less imposing Kendal.

Koretski held a Glock pistol in his left hand and the moment he saw Bolan he raised the weapon.

"Wait. We can still make this work, Cooper," he said, triggering his weapon. "There is…"

Bolan shot him in midsentence, the hefty boom of the Desert Eagle drowning out any words the Russian might have been saying. The trio of .357 mm slugs hammered him back across the room, blood spray dappling the carpet. The back of Koretski's legs caught a heavy coffee table and he pitched backward, the rear of his skull smashing against the edge of the stone hearth. He moved once, a wrenching spasm that turned his body on its side, then he became still.

Senator Tyrone Kendal seemed unable to draw his gaze from the blood-soaked body. He stared at the Russian, face suddenly drained of color. When he did move he looked at Bolan, shaking his head slightly.

"Time's up, Kendal."

"You won't kill me. I'm sure you've read up on who I am. The power I wield. My money. Position. I'm an important man."

"No," Bolan said. "You're an accessory to murder, a cheat and a man who has abused everything he's ever touched. A lot of people have suffered just because you dragged them into your grubby scheme. I've seen the depths you were prepared to go to protect yourself. The lives you messed with. And now you believe your position and money can buy you out of trouble."

"You forget I'm—"

"Untouchable? A U.S. senator?" Bolan allowed himself a cold, unfeeling smile. "You've used that one too many times, Kendal. The sell-by date has expired. And I'm not impressed, or intimidated."

The senator tried to make a run for it, grabbing Koretski's dropped pistol.

The Beretta whispered its disapproval, with two triple bursts that ended Kendal's life and sprayed his blood across the panoramic window behind him.

Bolan limped his way out of the death house and made his way back to where he had left his rifle. He picked up the brass casings and slipped them into a pocket. He took a transceiver from another pocket and keyed the button.

"Ready for pickup, Jack."

"Be there in ten, Sarge. You all squared away down there?"

"Yeah. Negotiations completed. I'm walking wounded down here, pal, so make it fast."

"Will do, Sarge. You hit bad?"

"I'll survive, but my pride took a little battering. Hell, Jack, I must be getting slow."

Grimaldi's laugh echoed from the speaker. "You? Slow? Sarge, you'll be telling me next that you're getting older."

Bolan lifted his face to the falling snow, feeling its cold touch on his skin. It felt good.

Older?

Yeah, maybe.
But what about wiser?
That was a question he wasn't sure he wanted to answer.

* * * * *

Don Pendleton's Mack Bolan

Road of Bones

A high-speed death chase through Russia's most brutal terrain

Dispatched on a high-priority search-and-rescue mission, Mack Bolan is on a motorcycle hell ride along the Road of Bones — a mass grave to thousands of slaves buried during Stalin's iron rule. It's a one-way trip effectively sealed at both ends by death squads. Every mile survived brings him closer to freedom...or certain doom.

Available April
wherever books are sold.

Or order your copy now by sending your name, address, zip or postal code, along with a check or money order (please do not send cash) for $6.99 for each book ordered ($7.99 in Canada), plus 75¢ postage and handling ($1.00 in Canada), payable to Gold Eagle Books, to:

In the U.S.
Gold Eagle Books
3010 Walden Avenue
P.O. Box 9077
Buffalo, NY 14269-9077

In Canada
Gold Eagle Books
P.O. Box 636
Fort Erie, Ontario
L2A 5X3

Please specify book title with your order.
Canadian residents add applicable federal and provincial taxes.

GOLD EAGLE ®

www.readgoldeagle.blogspot.com

GSB149R

TAKE 'EM FREE
2 action-packed novels plus a mystery bonus

NO RISK
NO OBLIGATION TO BUY

SPECIAL LIMITED-TIME OFFER
Mail to: The Reader Service

IN U.S.A.: P.O. Box 1867, Buffalo, NY 14240-1867
IN CANADA: P.O. Box 609, Fort Erie, Ontario L2A 5X3

YEAH! Rush me 2 FREE Gold Eagle® novels and my FREE mystery bonus (bonus is worth about $5). If I don't cancel, I will receive 6 hot-off-the-press novels every other month. Bill me at the low price of just $31.94 for each shipment.* That's a savings of at least 24% off the combined cover prices and there is NO extra charge for shipping and handling! There is no minimum number of books I must buy. I can always cancel at any time simply by returning a shipment at your cost or by returning any shipping statement marked "cancel." Even if I never buy another book, the 2 free books and mystery bonus are mine to keep forever.

166/366 ADN FEJF

Name	(PLEASE PRINT)	
Address		Apt. #
City	State/Prov.	Zip/Postal Code

Signature (if under 18, parent or guardian must sign)

Not valid to current subscribers of Gold Eagle books.
Want to try two free books from another series?
Call 1-800-873-8635 or visit www.ReaderService.com.

* Terms and prices subject to change without notice. Prices do not include applicable taxes. Sales tax applicable in N.Y. Canadian residents will be charged applicable taxes. Offer not valid in Quebec. This offer is limited to one order per household. All orders subject to credit approval. Credit or debit balances in a customer's account(s) may be offset by any other outstanding balance owed by or to the customer. Please allow 4 to 6 weeks for delivery. Offer available while quantities last.

Your Privacy—The Reader Service is committed to protecting your privacy. Our Privacy Policy is available online at www.ReaderService.com or upon request from the Reader Service.

We make a portion of our mailing list available to reputable third parties that offer products we believe may interest you. If you prefer that we not exchange your name with third parties, or if you wish to clarify or modify your communication preferences, please visit us at www.ReaderService.com/consumerschoice or write to us at Reader Service Preference Service, P.O. Box 9062, Buffalo, NY 14269. Include your complete name and address.

GE11B

JAMES AXLER

DEATH LANDS

Palaces of Light

JAMES AXLER

DEATH LANDS

Palaces of Light

A treacherous quest through tomorrow's post-nuclear reality.

A treacherous quest through tomorrow's post-nuclear reality.

Steeped in beauty and mysticism, the canyons of Mesa Verde, Colorado, survived the blast that altered the American West. Ryan Cawdor and his band follow the trail to a legendary city carved in stone, older and stronger than the nukecaust — the palaces of light. The inhabitants are masters of mind games, poised to push the companions over the edge....

Available May wherever books are sold.

Or order your copy now by sending your name, address, zip or postal code, along with a check or money order (please do not send cash) for $6.99 for each book ordered ($7.99 in Canada), plus 75¢ postage and handling ($1.00 in Canada), payable to Gold Eagle Books, to:

In the U.S.	**In Canada**
Gold Eagle Books	Gold Eagle Books
3010 Walden Avenue	P.O. Box 636
P.O. Box 9077	Fort Erie, Ontario
Buffalo, NY 14269-9077	L2A 5X3

Please specify book title with your order.
Canadian residents add applicable federal and provincial taxes.

GOLD EAGLE®

www.readgoldeagle.blogspot.com

GDL104R

AleX Archer
MAGIC LANTERN

A world steeped in magic...and a deadly curse.

In Lond... ...ward the
mysteri... ...ce used
...century
...e delves
...rk past
...ge. And
...harness
...cursed
...rything
...asures
...mises.

...e *May*
...e *sold.*

www.readgoldeagle.blogspot.com

GRA36R